Dangerous embrace

"Please let me go." Helen's eyes were no longer blue but deeply purple, locked with his.

"Are you sure?"

His voice held the edge of irony and his softly taunting attitude quickly dispelled the hazy cloud of wonder she floated on, shame coming immediately to take its place.

"I'm perfectly sure. I think I've had enough of your experiments, Mr. Maclean!"

"Don't be a fool, Helen!" he said quietly, suddenly angered. "If that was an experiment it was a very dangerous one to conduct in this empty house. You've got a very low opinion of yourself. I kissed you because it's the natural reaction when a very beautiful girl is in my arms and I stopped because my next natural reaction would have been to take things a good deal further."

PATRICIA WILSON used to live in Yorkshire, England, but with her children all grown up, she decided to give up her teaching position there and accompany her husband on an extended trip to Spain. Their travels are providing her with plenty of inspiration for her romance writing.

Books by Patricia Wilson

Don't miss any of our special offers. Write to us at the following address for information on our newest releases.

Harlequin Reader Service
P.O. Box 1397, Buffalo, NY 14240
Canadian address: P.O. Box 603,
Fort Erie, Ont. L2A 5X3

PATRICIA WILSON

Perilous Refuge

Harlequin Books

TORONTO • NEW YORK • LONDON
AMSTERDAM • PARIS • SYDNEY • HAMBURG
STOCKHOLM • ATHENS • TOKYO • MILAN
MADRID • WARSAW • BUDAPEST • AUCKLAND

Harlequin Presents first edition December 1992
ISBN 0-373-11518-7

Original hardcover edition published in 1991
by Mills & Boon Limited

PERILOUS REFUGE

CHAPTER ONE

'ROSS MACLEAN arrives from New York and takes over next week. So it's America for me in seven days. We'll pass in the night—like ships.'

Jim Saxton began to sing 'New York, New York' under his breath, busy at once with the documents Helen had placed on his desk. He was obviously delighted but Helen just stood there, a flare of dismay on her face, the announcement temporarily scrambling her mind.

This change-over had been in the air for some time but she had never really thought it would happen, never quite believed in it. The headquarters of Maclean International had seemed safely distant for one thing, the width of the Atlantic Ocean making changes unlikely, and Jim was not at all suited for life at the fast pace of New York. She knew that herself, so surely a driving company like Maclean International would know it? Helen had always secretly believed they would, that Jim had suffered from wishful thinking. She could see now that the wishful thinking had been hers alone. He was actually leaving in one week, her easygoing, accommodating boss. She didn't quite know what to say.

'I—I hope you enjoy it.' Her best wishes seemed totally inadequate alongside his euphoria, and she really wanted a few minutes alone to pull herself together.

'If I can wangle it, I'll never come back!'

It had the cold ring of finality about it and Helen managed a smile. So what was she going to do now? Her cosy little job seemed to be falling about her ears. The quiet wall she had built around herself did not now seem so safe and secure. She went to get the coffee. It was time for that anyway, and it gave her the much needed minute to think.

In her own, small office she put the coffee to percolate and stood watching it, her eyes lifting at last to look in the mirror that hung over the small oak table where she had prepared coffee for herself and her buoyant boss for the last two years. Brilliant blue eyes looked back at her, stunned with disbelief, her oval face with its fine, elegant bone-structure rather anxious.

Jim had been late this morning, a not unusual event—he came in as he pleased and, although it usually pleased him to be there, if he felt like coming in at ten he did so. It never bothered Helen. She had the running of the general manager's office down to a fine art; he only had to come in, slide into his chair and everything moved smoothly on well-oiled wheels. She anticipated his every wish, putting papers in his hand sometimes before he had asked a thing. It was a perfect working arrangement. There was just one stipulation—he never kept her late. At five o'clock Helen locked her desk and left. Jim Saxton understood and never transgressed. Would Ross Maclean understand? She doubted it, and she couldn't be flexible.

She knew that most of the other secretaries were often here until six-thirty or even seven, depending on the whim of their bosses, while she, secretary to the general manager himself, kept her own rules and her own hours. She couldn't expect that to continue now, not with the son of the founder of the giant firm taking over this office himself. She might very well be out of a job.

Helen smoothed her hair almost absently. Heavy and straight, almost blue-black, it hung to her shoulders and beyond, but at work it was severely curtailed, fastened in a thick braid that wound around her head in a shining coil. She touched a lip gloss to her smooth lips in a peculiar act of bravado and lifted the tray to take it back to Jim's office. She didn't feel very brave at the moment. Extremely uneasy would be satisfactory words to describe her feelings.

'When will he arrive?' It sounded a bit desperate, unlike the cool image she projected, and she hastily covered up. 'I mean, will he be here before you leave for America? I expect he'll want to see himself into the job.'

If Ross Maclean came before Jim left then maybe things would work out. Jim would explain their working relationship, although he would probably keep quiet about his own peculiar hours and his frequent forays to the golf course.

'I hope he doesn't arrive until I'm across the Atlantic,' Jim muttered, sipping hot coffee. 'Ross Maclean, my dear Helen, is the source of all energy, the ultimate dynamo, power and drive in its raw state. He doesn't ease himself into anything, he explodes into it. Heaven help us if he comes here before I've left—he'll give me a nervous breakdown, *then* he'll sack me!'

'We're efficient,' Helen said resentfully, shivering at the description of her future boss. She got a rueful look from laughing eyes.

'You're efficient, Miss Andrews. I'm a con man. If I don't come up with someone like you in New York I'll be sent packing. You're the perfect front.' His eyes slid over her figure. 'The perfect everything actually, though I tell you this at this late stage in our relationship, knowing as I do that you're a confirmed nun in disguise.'

'Will he want me, though?' Helen asked, too worried to banter.

'Don't we all?' Jim laughed at her suddenly flushed face and relented. She was a sweetly beautiful girl but utterly unapproachable. His attempts in the past had received nothing but a look of blue-eyed astonishment. It showed she was unsettled that she even blushed. 'Honestly, Helen, as far as I know he'll keep the whole place intact. He may not even stay. I think this is what's called a whim, his father's whim. Go forth and snoop! He leads a fast and furious life over there. Here he'll die of boredom. He's probably as annoyed about this as you are.'

'I'm not annoyed,' Helen assured him quickly.

'Just worried?' He looked at her levelly. 'I'm not quite the idiot I seem. I know you've got problems, even though you don't talk about them.'

Helen hedged him away from the subject of her problems. She never discussed her private life. 'You're the best boss I've ever had.'

'Not many of those in your twenty-four years, so I won't let it go to my head. Try not to worry,' he added quietly, his laughter dying. 'You'll manage Ross Maclean as well as you've managed me, and if he lets you go he's not at all like his old man. Old Maclean can see straight through people. His son looks at you as if he could drill into your mind with his eyes, so he's probably a chip off the old block. He'll appreciate your worth.'

If that was supposed to calm her, then it had failed sadly. Jim Saxton hadn't exactly painted a picture of human kindness, and he should know. It wasn't more than two weeks since he had flown to New York to see the set-up there. He'd looked a little shattered when he returned but Helen had put this down to the long flight. Now she wasn't too sure. She didn't want to work with a man who could drill holes into her mind with his eyes. She despised hard men. One brute in a lifetime was enough for anyone.

Helen was still mulling the problem over as she got off the bus and walked along the quiet road to the small cottage at the far end. It was the dark time of the year when even small problems seemed to be enlarged out of all proportion. The street lights cast long shadows, emphasising the darkness around, and there were flurries of snow, the odd white flake settling on her black hair. It was bitterly cold with the year fast approaching its end. There might even be snow for Christmas. It seemed a good time, actually, for the arrival of trouble.

She quickened her steps. It was almost five-thirty. Tina had to leave in an hour. Their timing was always immaculate and if it ever failed on any regular basis then she would have to find another job. Tina had suffered enough and nothing would be allowed to change their arrangements. Finding another job with the same good salary would be a bit tricky, though, and she wouldn't have time to search around much. Money was tight and getting tighter.

Helen let herself into the cottage, its warm atmosphere closing around her, a little of her gloom falling away as she heard voices, Tina talking at her usual speed, Tansy trying to get a word in. There was a delicious smell wafting across from the kitchen and she smiled to herself. They had sorted out their lives after all. They had made this atmosphere and nothing was going to intrude.

'I'm home!' Helen tossed her bag on to the table in the hall and just managed to get her coat on to a chair before a small bundle of energy hit her. Jim had said that Ross Maclean was the source of all energy—not quite, she had her own private source. She scooped her three-year-old daughter up into her arms and turned her laughing face to the kitchen door as her sister appeared, grinning widely.

'Greetings, chief!' Tina waved a wooden spoon and bowed. 'Tea's in the pot, dinner's on the cooker.' They both looked at the clock in the hall, the hands exactly on five-thirty.

'It's half-past five,' Tansy's bubbling voice announced and they all laughed.

'I'm not sure this ritual is good for her,' Helen said in amusement. 'She'll probably grow up thinking that something momentous should happen at five-thirty each day.'

'It does,' Tina said firmly, relieving Helen of her cuddly burden. 'Mummy comes home from the big world of business.'

'May she continue to do so,' Helen prayed in a fervent mutter, following Tina into the kitchen.

'Trouble?'

'Maybe.' Helen poured herself a much needed cup of tea and sat down on one of the stools, heaving Tansy back on to her lap. 'I can't really believe it yet, but Jim got his transfer after all. Ross Maclean is coming over to take his place—at least, he'll be here temporarily.'

'The big white chief here? The Maclean of Maclean's?' Tina's face was a picture of disbelief.

'The son and heir.' Helen's arched brows rose fractionally. 'Jim thinks he may be on a snooping expedition for the old man.'

'How long have we got to return the spoons?' Tina questioned with a wide grin, but Helen's face put a stop to that.

'Honestly, it's no laughing matter. Jim seems to go in dread of him. He says that Ross Maclean can drill holes with his eyes.'

'Hard,' Tina mused, checking the cooking.

'Granite. Anyway, he'll be here in a week, and if he doesn't like my time-keeping trouble will ensue. I may very well have to start looking for another job.'

'I could pack in the course,' Tina offered quickly, getting herself a severe look for her pains. Helen glanced at her watch.

'Get moving. We'll eat when you're ready.'

'OK.' Tina drifted out of the kitchen and Helen collected an apron, tying it around her slender waist and turning more attention to her daughter.

'What did you do today, darling?'

'Everything!'

Helen looked down at the small replica of herself and smiled. Tansy was perfect, eyes the same blue as her own, blue that could change suddenly to purple, hair the same shining black but packed in soft curls around her small face. She felt the sharp band of pain, the same old fear for one second, a fiercely protective urge in her to pick Tansy up and squeeze her tightly. There was nothing of Miles in Tansy—nothing! It might have been an immaculate conception in the way that Tansy mirrored only herself.

'You said to me it's rude to stare,' Tansy pointed out a little worriedly, and Helen's face relaxed into smiles.

'So it is, but I haven't seen you all day. I'm just looking.'

'Can I stay up late, then?'

'A bit,' Helen conceded readily, knowing quite well that Tansy would be ready for bed at the appropriate time. A day with Tina was enough to wear out anyone, and Tansy used up the same sort of energy.

'I can't see why there should be trouble,' Tina remarked later as they ate. 'I know the hours are supposed to be nine till five-thirty but you go in early to make up for it. Anyway, maybe we could adjust our own time-table if this Maclean chap kicks up rough?'

'We've been through this,' Helen sighed, bending to rescue Tansy's spoon. 'I leave at five. I get here at five-thirty. That gives you one hour to get ready, eat and go. You're not giving up the course, Tina. You would be at university now if everything were as it ought to be.'

'Dad wanted you to go to university too, even though you did decide a bit late,' Tina pointed out quietly and Helen dismissed it with a shrug.

'It didn't work out like that.' She glanced at the clock. 'You'll miss the bus.'

'Helen. Couldn't we...?'

'Begone!' Helen stood and scooped up Tansy, and her sister grinned as she made for the door.

'Yes, chief!'

It was always the same, this light-hearted banter. Time was when they had both been completely light-hearted, nothing seeming able to touch the happy circle that was family. But tragedy had struck with bewildering speed, their parents were killed in a motorway crash, and they had salvaged what they could of their lives.

Tina had been fifteen then, still at school, and Helen had been twenty, only just twenty, her birthday the day before the tragedy. It had been easy for Miles Gilford to persuade Helen into marriage, his loving sympathy, his concern for their future, his assurance that Tina would have a home with them and go to university all adding to his already charming presence.

Handsome, clever, gentle, he had seemed too good to be true. He was! It had only been because of her father's carefully worded will that Helen and Tina now had a roof over their heads. He had not liked Miles at all, his opposition to Helen seeing Miles the only cloud that had ever come between herself and her parents. How right her father had been.

Helen shook off this brooding mood. She rarely brooded about it now. She was much too busy. At first, keeping busy had been a necessity, a way to recover from the horror her marriage had become. Now it was habit as well as necessity. She was the bread-winner, head of this small family unit, the chief!

With Tansy in bed, and thankful to go, Helen sat down to have a few minutes' rest, her mind instantly returning to her work situation. As secretary to the English general manager of a huge, international electronics firm she was well paid and secure, or had been. Tina was taking evening classes until next year. Her final years at school had been too traumatic for her to do as well as she should, and the necessary A Levels had to be gained. Next year she would get into university, at least one of them fulfilling their parents' wishes, although belatedly. In any case, Tina was clever and deserved the chance. She had a flair for languages. Helen was proud of her, and almost obsessively protective as she was with Tansy. It was only natural, or so she repeatedly told herself.

What if Ross Maclean made life difficult? She had never seen him, only heard about him. Like his father, he had a reputation for keen business acumen and harsh personal relationships. The days of a buoyant boss were over. Maybe he wouldn't stay? He could hardly be thinking of staying permanently in England. Jim had been more than impressed with the lifestyle of Ross Maclean in New York. Glamorous women and fast cars, he had said flippantly, but she had seen the small flare of envy there.

There wasn't much hope for that sort of thing in this town—even a fast car would be sorely overdoing it. The possibility of his staying for more than a few weeks was slim. He might even announce his departure date as he arrived. This was small cheese to him. It wasn't even London. Snoop and then put another man in would probably be his orders. If she kept her head down, played it softly, she would be left in peace. Jim might even be sent back when they realised how unsuited he was for the cut and thrust of American business.

Helen sighed and hauled herself to her feet. She would wash the dishes and then have a long bath. Her eye fell on the calendar in the kitchen and she had to restrain herself from marking off the days. One week. There was nothing she could do about it. They would have to wait and see. She couldn't seem to get the name of Ross Maclean out of her mind.

The week flew. It hadn't been a good week for anyone and Helen felt guilty when she realised that her own well-hidden anxiety had not allowed her to be extra kind to Jim Saxton. He was having nerves of his own and she hadn't helped. She had been busy all week trying to make an efficient arrangement more efficient still until Jim had complained that Ross Maclean didn't need to come at all. He could simply telephone from New York each day and fax a few letters.

'Honestly, Helen, with you here and going at this pace, who needs a general manager?'

'I'm only——'

'Working yourself into a breakdown? Ease off. He'll not eat you. I mean, somebody must love him, even if it's only his mother.'

'Has he got a mother?' Helen flushed at her own stupid remark and Jim grinned widely.

'Well, it's only a rumour. He must have come from somewhere though.'

Now, with Monday upon her and the day of reck-oning at hand, Helen hurried into the offices of Maclean International and took the lift to the top floor. It was eight-thirty, on the dot, nobody in the building yet except the caretaker. She would be able to get the letters out, slide into her routine and be quite prepared for trouble when it arrived. He might not get in until late—after all, he would have only arrived last night if Jim's surmising was correct. There had been a conference in Boston and Jim knew that Ross Maclean had been there until Saturday. He would have to get his hotel sorted out too.

By the time she had taken off her coat, glanced at the mail on her desk and looked at herself critically in the mirror, she had persuaded herself that he wouldn't be here today at all. A reprieve. She had gone to extra trouble today to look efficient, her grey suit and red blouse neatly tailored, her black hair more severe than usual. It seemed a bit of a waste now, the extra effort.

She walked through to check his office for faults all the same, just to be on the safe side, and her heart bounded in her chest like an agitated ball as a tall figure unwound itself from the chair to about six-foot-two high, piercing grey eyes leaping at her, almost pinning her to the door. A wave of involuntary shock hit her and for a moment she stood there dry-mouthed, rooted to the spot.

He was aggressively handsome, no sign of softness about him at all, and no sign of humour either. Dark, tanned, his impossibly light eyes now narrowed and compelling, his tall, lean height seemed to hold in a powerful hostility. She couldn't seem to do anything but stare, looking back into eyes like silver ice. Jim's words slid foolishly through her mind—'He must have come from somewhere'—a granite quarry? Ross Maclean might well have been fashioned from rock by a master craftsman. He didn't seem quite human. His assessing contemplation of her made Helen feel utterly insignificant, and panic slid over her like a wet sheet.

'Miss Andrews?' He perched easily on the edge of the desk, his gaze going over her steadily as if she were company property that he might decide to trade off against better equipment. He glanced at the paper in his hand. 'Apparently, your—late boss, felt the need to leave me a brief on you. It's interesting. Your qualifications are superb, your excellence above reproach. The footnote is touching.' He glanced down, his mouth twisting sardonically as he read Jim's words aloud. '"Left to herself, she is capable of running the office smoothly and efficiently. Her personal problems never interfere with her work. She responds to gentle handling."'

She was listening to his voice, a compelling voice, darkly seductive in spite of the disparagement, like black velvet over steel. He looked up, his eyes silver flares of light, and he said nothing at all, simply waiting for Helen to get control of her breathing, her blushes and her astonishment.

'He—er—I can't think why... Jim has a strange sense of humour,' she finished lamely.

'Jim does?' he enquired softly, his voice cold behind the velvet tone, evidently affronted that she called her 'late boss' by his first name. 'I hope it holds out in New York. As you seem to run everything, the workload that's going to hit him over there may kill him.'

There was the implied threat that if the workload didn't kill Jim then Ross Maclean very well might, and Helen sprang to his defence.

'I assume, Mr Maclean, that he was trying to make things a little easier for me. He's probably left all the staff files for you—er—to hand.'

'Only yours, Miss Andrews. It seems he wanted to be sure that I continued where he left off—handling you gently.'

He placed a lot of emphasis on the word 'handling', and Helen's renewed blushes did nothing to help, nor did the flare of resentment in her eyes, their purple shade now more pronounced. It seemed to snap his attention more closely to her.

'I don't need handling at all, Mr Maclean.' Anger began to surface inside her, slowly but very surely. Oh, she knew men like this! 'I came for your mail,' she continued, coolly. 'Normally I'm the only one here at this time in the morning. In future, I'll knock.'

'A slight tap will do.' He sat down, tossing the paper to the back of his desk. 'I've been through my mail already, Miss Andrews. Get the rest done and then you can take the replies for this lot.'

'Very well, Mr Maclean.' Helen's hand hovered over the embarrassing paper. She wanted to snatch it up and his glance rested on her slender fingers, his lips twisting ironically. 'Shall I file this?'

'Definitely not, Miss Andrews.' She was at the receiving end of that punishing stare again. 'I'll keep it to hand. Top drawer. I have to learn it yet, especially the postscript. I'll follow the general guidelines until I work out my own method of handling.'

Helen looked down at him in irritation but he seemed to be towering menacingly even when he was seated and she gave an exasperated sigh, her slender figure bristling with indignation as she walked out. She might not even last the day. Hostility had arrived and it had arrived at least half an hour before her. What would happen at five o'clock? It would be a relief to be dismissed, if she didn't need the money so much, because she could tell right now that she was not going to be able to get on at

all with Ross Maclean. She was wary of his granite
hardness but she refused to be afraid. She would never
be afraid of a man again, never in her whole life!

She finished with her usual speed and walked back to
his office, giving the suggested slight tap. He was on the
phone and nodded her to a seat, his face still set in the
uncompromising hard lines. It gave her the chance to
watch him surreptitiously. He must be about thirty-five,
his hair very dark brown, his lips almost carved but more
sensuous than bitter in spite of his harsh exterior. He
had that look of easy wealth about him that was never
possible to achieve by acting. She should know—Miles
had tried hard enough to look like a wealthy business-
man and failed miserably. There was nothing of Miles
in this man.

Helen snapped to attention as she realised that the call
was finished and he was looking at her too, his eyes like
polished crystal.

'You find me peculiar, Miss Andrews?' The voice was
deep, disturbing, and Helen had to fight hard to keep
cool.

'I was listening to your voice,' she improvised. 'You're
not an American, Mr Maclean?'

'That surprises you? I don't see why it should. The
parent company is in America but I'm English, so is my
father, although my mother is American. I was educated
here. My father likes to keep his roots firmly planted.'

'I wasn't prying. I was just—thinking.'

Helen raised her pencil in a businesslike manner and
assumed a prim look. The carved lips twitched a little.

'Quite natural, surely? Working so closely together,
we'll have to size each other up.' He leaned back in his
chair, apparently not yet ready to start. 'Why were you
in so early?'

The words were shot at her like bullets and she stiffened at once. Here it came, she might as well face it at once.

'I always come in at eight-thirty because I have to leave at five.'

'*Have* to? Is that part of the gentle handling?'

'It's the arrangement I made when I started here. It's always been honoured.'

Her tone of voice did not amuse him and she found herself once more pinned by his gaze.

'I work late sometimes, Miss Andrews. What happens then?'

'It's all right if it's Wednesday.' Some of the colour had left her face. Her hands were beginning to shake in spite of her determination not to be intimidated, and the eagle eyes missed nothing; they flashed to her face, drifting over it.

'We'll see.' He dismissed the subject and got right down to dictation, but each time she looked up he was watching her closely, although the deep, dark voice never faltered. Clearly his mind wasn't entirely on what he was doing. When she came to type it up she was impressed. So he could think of several things at one and the same time? She had the nasty feeling that his brainwaves were invading her office and it kept her glancing continuously at the door. By the end of the day she was wound up like a wire.

'I'm leaving now, Mr Maclean.' Helen stood for a moment in his doorway, her coat on to prove her point, but he hardly glanced up.

'Very well, Miss Andrews. Goodnight.'

His cool politeness was worse than a slap, his acceptance of her prompt departure somehow coldly dismissive, and she felt her face flooding with colour. He had kept her on edge all day and now he was calmly accepting her right to go, but it wasn't the end of the subject. She knew that surely.

The dark head was once again bent to his papers and when she stood hesitantly watching him he looked up, one dark eyebrow quirked at her, a disturbing gleam at the back of his eyes. She just nodded and went, realising that he had got right under her skin with very few words. She felt hot and flustered, quite shaky actually. It lasted all the way home, her wound-up nerves making her feel almost ill.

'How did it go?'

Tina looked as anxious as she felt and Helen made a wry face.

'Badly, I think. He's pretty awful.' They had dispensed with the usual entry routine and Tansy was watching with great interest.

'What does he look like?' Tina wanted to know, and Helen was quite astonished how clearly a picture of him sprang into her head. No doubt he could listen from a distance and was transmitting the picture.

'Handsome, wealthy and hard—cruelly hard,' she added almost defiantly, her lips tightening as she realised just how much he had got under her skin. She still looked shaken and Tina frowned, her hot temper surfacing.

'You're not to put up with one single thing! You hear me, Helen? Those days are gone.'

'I know,' Helen agreed warily. 'Come on. You'll be late.'

'The class is cancelled for tonight,' Tina assured her with a grin. 'I had a phone call.'

'Thank goodness.' Helen sank into a chair. 'I feel worn out.'

'Not getting a migraine?' Tina was instantly anxious but Helen shook her head and gratefully took a cup of tea.

'No. I just got worked up. It's ridiculous really. After all, he didn't do anything but work. He didn't object when I left. It's just that... Oh, I don't know.'

She did know really, deep down. She was afraid of Ross Maclean's hardness. Miles was a blustering bully—after she had got away, after the divorce, she had come to see that. If she had stood up to him, not been so cowed, he would never have dared to treat her as he had done. Ross Maclean, though, was naturally hard, not a chink in his armour, and every signal inside her had flashed, every defence mechanism had come to red alert. She had been unconsciously defending herself from the moment she had seen him. How soon he would leave was the thing uppermost in her mind as she went to bed.

If it hadn't been for the effect he had on her, Helen would have been fascinated by the week that followed. Maclean International was a very powerful company, doing business with almost every country in Western Europe as well as the United States and most of the South American countries. Their products and expertise were greatly in demand and this base in England was very small fry at the side of the American parent company.

Even so, with the advent of Ross Maclean, a very subtle change came over things. Calls began to come in from all over the world. The balance of power seemed to have tilted across the Atlantic and Helen's workload doubled. In the space of one week she seemed to develop her efficiency to the point of frantic activity, more and more of her everyday work having to be delegated to the typing pool. He noticed.

CHAPTER TWO

ON FRIDAY Helen found Ross Maclean there, ahead of her as usual, and instead of answering when she offered him a polite and cool 'good morning' he frowned down at her thoughtfully.

'This can't go on. At this rate, you'll need a skateboard.'

'I don't quite know...?'

'Stop fencing, Miss Andrews.' His gaze seemed to gain concentration, stabbing at her. 'You and I are on the same wavelength. We both know that this week your work has increased unbearably. It will grow. You need an assistant.'

Helen just stared at him, her mind racing. An assistant! Where would this person go? Her own office was small. It would take away her bit of privacy, crack her small wall of safety.

'But—but how? I mean...another secretary couldn't fit in and my office is so small...'

'Why does change frighten you? You guard your little nest, don't you?' His astute assessment of her state of mind gave her a swift pang of uneasiness again, the narrowed eyes like twin points of light, a kind of alarming recognition in them. 'You're a very private person. I even feel like an intruder if I step one foot inside your domain.'

His ability to pick up her atmosphere didn't really shock her. His mind always seemed to be probing hers. Defence was automatic.

'I can tackle the work,' Helen stated firmly, more firmly than she felt.

'Oh, no, you can't. What do you propose? Come in at seven each day? There's a limit to how much of an early bird you can be. I'm afraid the rest of the world starts at nine and finishes at five-thirty.'

So that was it. A roundabout way of getting rid of her. Oddly enough, it disappointed her. She would have thought he would come straight out with things and not sneak up.

'You could dismiss me and get a more amenable secretary,' she said hotly, glaring at him. The dark brows rose slowly, his lips turned down in disparaging amusement.

'Don't be foolish, Miss Andrews. Come for a walk.'

The hand that gripped her arm lightly was as cool as his voice but Helen knew better than to pull away. There was a warning that spread from his fingertips and she found herself going to the lift, glancing anxiously at his hard profile as he jabbed the button for the next floor up.

'There are store-rooms up here, nothing else.'

Her breathless words merely brought a curt nod and he simply motioned her out as the lift stopped at the very top of the building, opening straight into a huge room that spread over the entire floor.

Helen had never actually been up here before. If she wanted anything then one of the clerks delivered it to her after a brief call. The whole place was stacked with various types of office equipment: typing paper, continuous paper for the word processors, ribbons, disks, boxes and boxes of equipment that had been stored here for years, some apparently from the firm who had owned the building before them. There were typewriters now hopelessly outdated and she could even see her old chair, one that had been very uncomfortable and had been replaced a year ago.

'Inefficient use of space.' Ross Maclean's voice was very deep and quiet in the huge room. 'Good light, though.' He nodded to the big windows in the roof, sloping and more than adequate.

'You're proposing to turn this into an office?' Some comment seemed to be expected and Helen turned wide blue eyes on him.

'Offices.' His gaze ran over her for a second, from her eyes to her black hair. His brief inspection stopped at her high tilted breasts and she felt a panicky flare of feeling, her cheeks flushing swiftly. His eyes returned to hers, curiously intent for a second, and then he began to pace about, his hands in his pockets.

'I came up here last night. I've got the plan more or less worked out in my mind. I'll have somebody in on Monday to look the place over and they can get started. I imagine we'll get three offices out of this—mine, yours and your assistant's. You can advertise for her today and interview as soon as possible, unless there's someone in the building already you care to promote?'

He had ushered her back into the lift before she came to her senses.

'I . . . You want me to be the one who decides?'

'Naturally.' He leaned against the panelling of the lift and looked at her quizzically. 'This is your assistant, not mine. Her office will be tacked on to yours and, with a bit of luck, I'll hardly see her. She eases your burden, you ease mine. Normal procedure.'

'But . . .' Helen followed him into his office as they came to their own floor. To say she was surprised was putting it mildly.

'You don't feel capable of dealing with this, Miss Andrews?'

'Of course I do!' His suddenly derisive glance annoyed her and she gave him a small, fierce glare that shot sparks.

'Then stop clucking at my heels and get on with it.'

Really! He was impossible. Helen retreated, closing his door firmly, but she had the decided feeling that she had missed something in all this. A mind like that was never straightforward. He really *must* be up to something.

'So have you been promoted?' Tina wanted to know that night when Helen disclosed this latest upheaval.

'No. I'm not sure what's happened. On the surface everything's normal and it's quite true that I'm run off my feet, but I've just got the feeling that things aren't quite what they seem, as if I'm standing on a slippery deck.'

'Maybe when you've got the new person trained he'll get rid of you?' Tina suggested darkly, and Helen had to admit it had entered her mind.

'Who will you get?'

'Probably Jeanette from the typing pool. She's good. I get on well enough with her and if she has to be crammed in with me until this new place is ready then at least I can bear it. I'll see her on Monday. I'm for bed.'

Even though she was terribly tired, Helen had a lot of trouble sleeping. Ross Maclean seemed to hang around in her mind and, although she had no evidence at all, she realised she was projecting sinister meanings into almost everything he did. Whether it was fair or not didn't seem to matter. He was too compelling to be taken at face value, an opposing force that made an ordinary event seem two-edged.

* * *

Jeanette was overjoyed on Monday to be informed that she could try out for the new job as Helen's assistant. She was a petite blonde, her appearance almost the exact opposite to Helen's slender height and cool dark beauty. Ross Maclean looked at Helen with raised brows as Jeanette left to spread her good tidings around the lower offices.

'Snow White and Rose Red. Are you sure you know what you're doing, Miss Andrews?'

Helen felt a flare of annoyance at his dry comment. 'Yes. Jeanette knows what she's doing too,' she said stiffly. 'She's quite used to working with me. Most of my extra work usually ends up on her desk.'

'She looks a bit frivolous.' His lips quirked, his mind no doubt lingering on Jeanette's short blonde hair, which owed a great deal to a bottle, her curvy figure and her fierce blushes as she had met the boss.

'I think she was overcome,' Helen murmured sarcastically, surprising herself. 'She doesn't often get the chance to meet really important people.'

She knew it was nasty but he brought out the worst in her, and she didn't like the way he constantly made little digs at her either.

'I'm sure you'll soon put her at ease,' he murmured as drily, 'or whip her into shape.'

'No doubt.' Helen's phone began to ring and his phone was ringing too. The day had started with its usual rush and her comments went unpunished, but she didn't miss the gleam in his eyes. Why did she feel it necessary to fight with him? He hadn't done anything wrong, after all. He was simply being what he was: a hard, remote male, too powerful and too sardonic to be human. She realised that she had never once smiled at him. Her only hope was to be aloof, and she hung on to her dignity with a grim determination. How many times had he smiled at her, come to think of it? None. His attitude was utterly dismissive. If he softened at all it was to bend sufficiently to be scornful. Her work situation had deteriorated from the moment he had arrived here. She was unsettled all the time.

His lack of humanity became more apparent at the end of the day. Jeanette was to begin the next morning and, as five o'clock drew near, Helen realised grudgingly that Ross Maclean was quite right, she *did* need an assistant. This day had been much more than hectic for both of them. His phone was ringing now and she prayed hers wouldn't. She watched it warily as she started to put her things away.

'Miss Andrews.'

Helen jumped as his voice came over the intercom, her stomach muscles tightening as she felt the usual churning inside at the sound of his voice, the peculiar way he said her name. Now what? She took a few deep breaths before going in there. It was ten to five, she couldn't stand about chatting or she would miss the bus.

'You'll have to stay tonight. I've just had Paris on the line and I've got to get a letter off to them in tonight's post.' He wasn't looking at her as she stood in his doorway. He was rifling through papers on his desk as he threw the words crisply at her and it was a second before he looked up and saw that she had made no move.

'The letter, Miss Andrews.' The black brows rose in irritated surprise. 'Let's get on with it. It has to go in the late post.'

'I leave at five, Mr Maclean,' she said quietly, glancing at her watch. 'I did explain to you.'

'Explain be damned! This is an emergency!' He stood, his hands flat on the surface of his desk, his whole body leaning forward with unwarranted menace, and Helen's cheeks paled. She hated rows, she couldn't cope with them. He hadn't finished either. 'I will *try* to curtail the times when I need you after five. I will *try* to handle you gently. This time, however, I need you and you'll stay!'

'I can't.' Helen looked at him as steadily as she could, her eyes vividly blue, and his own crystal-grey eyes darkened threateningly.

'May I remind you that you work for Maclean International and your duty is first and foremost to the firm. In America you would work all hours that heaven sent, but even here the firm takes precedence over evenings with the boyfriend!'

'It does not take precedence over my duty at home,' she said quietly. 'I can't let it do that.'

Her hands were shaking again but this time he didn't know because she slid them into the pockets of her smart suit, her fingernails painfully thrust against her palms. She would never again break down in front of a man and she kept her lips in one straight line, her whole attitude appearing to be unbending when in fact she was desperately trying not be afraid of male anger.

'Duty at home?' He looked astonished and on the point of explosion. He straightened up, his towering height threatening her more. 'You can come in at nine tomorrow, Miss Andrews. Leave the dishes in the sink tonight and get to them in the morning, how about that?' he suggested sarcastically. 'As to the boyfriend, phone him and explain.'

'There's nothing to explain, Mr Maclean, because I'm not staying. My duty at home is my small daughter. Even you must see that she can't be left in the sink to wait until I'm free. She's three years old and I have no baby-sitter after five-thirty. If I don't leave at five, I miss my bus. Whatever you say or decide to do, I intend to leave.'

If she hadn't been so upset, Helen would have laughed at the astonished expression on that harsh face. Apparently nobody had ever stood up to him before. She hoped the shock would kill him but he soon recovered, every line of his face deepening, his mouth tightening to one grim line.

His eyes flashed to her fingers, to the lack of rings, just checking again no doubt, and his expression was exactly the expression she had seen in so many eyes when her ringless fingers were noticed in connection with Tansy. She was an unmarried mother as far as everyone knew. The realisation of that fact often brought a very speculating look to male eyes. Ross Maclean's look was not speculating. He looked at her with contempt.

'I see. Then don't let me keep you, Miss Andrews.'

Helen turned and left, but the cold dismissal upset her more than she could have imagined. As she left she heard him calling down to the typing pool, asking for Jeanette, and she felt quite cold inside, worthless. He had managed to convey utter contempt with no words at all. Those grey eyes had dismissed her, written her off. When she got home she held herself tightly in check until Tina had left and Tansy was safely tucked up in bed, then she cried.

She cried with anger and resentment and a ridiculous feeling of hurt. She could have left her wedding-ring on and saved herself a lot of trouble, she had always known that, but after the divorce she had had to get it off her finger. It had been like a weight to drag her down, to drag all of them down. Let him think what he liked. Why should she care, after all? He was nothing to her, a stranger who would go before too long. Ships that passed in the night, as Jim had said.

What Ross Maclean thought was apparent. For the rest of the week he was more polite than he had ever been and more cold, if that was possible. She could feel the underlying contempt constantly there, looking up sometimes to find his frowning gaze on her as if he was trying to come up with some method of getting rid of her. He deliberately spoke to Jeanette, who was now settled into the office close to Helen. His way of avoiding contact with Helen even brought speculating looks from Jeanette, who was not known for her brilliant brainpower.

On Friday afternoon he came into the office and stood there until she could have screamed. Then he sent Jeanette off upstairs on what Helen knew at once was a wild-goose chase. The noise of the alterations had been abominable all week and it had only added to her already tightly strung nerves. Now he wanted quiet words with her.

She tensed up and faced him. What was this, the sack or a moral lecture? She dreaded either of those things. She needed this job or she would have left already, and if he said anything about her private affairs she was going to either shout or cry because he had driven her to the very end of her tether, his unbending attitude hurtful and cold.

Her eyes were wide and unknowingly vulnerable, her pale face looking far too young, and that fact seemed to irritate him. He stared at her for a second and then frowned, evidently working out how to tell her the worst.

'Tomorrow, I'm flying to Paris,' he suddenly bit out. 'I'll be there overnight and return Sunday morning.'

So what now? Was he going to say, 'Be out of here before I get back'? Helen said nothing and he looked at her determinedly.

'I want you to go with me, and don't tell me you can't, Miss Andrews,' he snapped. 'It's a meeting with Middle East buyers and very important. I need you there because you're a first-class secretary and have everything at your fingertips. If you can't get a baby-sitter for your daughter then, damn it all, we'll take her with us!'

Helen sat and looked at him, her astonishment written right across her face, and he glared down at her. She always looked supremely efficient, as efficient as she was. In her plum-coloured suit, her white blouse and with her hair braided on top of her head, she was the picture of the ideal private secretary. Except that now her lips were softly parted in shock, her eyes wide open, purple shadows dancing across the clear blue.

'Well?' His voice was irascible and Helen gulped, finding her voice.

'All right. If—if you could give me details...'

'What about your little girl?'

Helen looked away, feeling very burdened by the piercing quality of those grey eyes. She seemed to have very few defences against him, her normal defences not working at all any more.

'It's all right at the weekend. I don't like leaving her but I can get away with no difficulty. If you really need me——'

'I wouldn't be asking you if I didn't,' he snarled. He glanced at his watch. 'I have to go out, book us both on to the earliest flight possible for Paris tomorrow— first class. I'll deal with the hotel accommodation when I get back.' He turned to leave, as angry apparently as if she had said she wouldn't go. Maybe he had been hoping she would refuse so that he could fire her on the spot? 'You'll need clothes.' His glance flared over her suit.

'I have clothes, Mr Maclean,' Helen informed him stiffly. Her cheeks were burning at his glance and his lips tightened.

'You're the model of propriety, Miss Andrews,' he murmured sarcastically. 'However, Paris requires something special. I'll write you a cheque.'

'I *have* clothes, Mr Maclean!' Annoyed and embarrassed at his tone, Helen stood up and glared right back at him. The model of propriety in her dress but not in her private life—his scathing voice had said it all. 'I can assure you that Paris will not be shocked!'

For a second his eyes narrowed, a flare of admiration at the back of them; even so, she felt that he wanted to hurt her, only his hard-headed command of himself keeping him in check. His mouth suddenly quirked with the nearest thing to real amusement she had seen, but her blue eyes glared at him and he simply nodded, turning at the last minute to add,

'You'll need an evening dress too.' When she nodded stiffly, he called his parting shot. 'Do something about that hair or they may think you're my housekeeper.'

If the word processor hadn't been too heavy she would have heaved it after him. Jeanette came weaving back into the room on her high heels and caught the expression on Helen's face. Ross Maclean had almost bowled her over on his way out, not even noticing her even though she had smiled brilliantly at him.

'Been having a row?'

'No,' Helen said tightly. 'We're going to Paris tomorrow.'

'Ooh, la la!'

Jeanette got the benefit of Helen's newly acquired ability to glare.

'Shut up!' she spat, and Jeanette got right down to work.

Tina was open-mouthed when Helen got home and related the latest office news.

'Paris? But that's wonderful—isn't it?'

'It is not!' Helen had rushed straight upstairs, their timetable forgotten in her rage, and now she began to throw clothes on to her bed, her body shaking with resentment. 'I hate him! I hate him!' She turned on Tina with furious eyes. 'Do you know he said I look like a housekeeper? He as much as told me to cut my hair!'

'He wouldn't have the cheek!'

'He's got cheek enough for just about anything, *and* he thinks I'm an unmarried mother!'

'You enlightened him, of course?'

'No, I didn't. Why should I?' Helen raised her head proudly and Tina watched her in surprise. She had never seen her sister looking so beautiful nor so utterly furious. Normally, Helen was almost too quiet and even-tempered.

'Calm down. Let's eat.'

'I'd choke!'

'Then come and choke while I'm there. I can pound your back. I'm not standing about arguing. I have a class to attend!' She opened the bedroom door and refused to budge until Helen went down, her annoyance still simmering and her pride sorely wounded.

When Tina had gone and Tansy was safely in bed, Helen went back to pack her clothes. She was not short of clothes. Miles had kept up a good front, making sure that her outward appearance did not betray the humiliation she suffered in private. She had kept the clothes. She was too frugal to throw expensive garments away and though she had never had cause to wear them she took them out now and looked them over. It was quite fitting that they should be worn when she was with another hard, cruel male.

She frowned at herself in the mirror. He wasn't like Miles in any way. It was unfair to make any comparison,

and although she didn't feel inclined to be fair to Ross
Maclean she had to admit if only to herself that he was
worlds above men like Miles Gilford. He was a natural
part of his world, power and dominance sitting easily
on him. He was a formidable man, ruthless, but he would
never physically hurt a woman, instinctively she knew
that, even though she had also felt his desire to hurt her
in some way this very afternoon.

It was bitterly cold outside and she had to plan carefully what she would take. Something warm for travel.
Something sophisticated for the hotel and then an
evening dress. It didn't take long to decide and she remembered with annoyance that she was supposed to get
a bus to the office and meet him there tomorrow—very
early. He had offered clothes. He might have offered a
taxi. It would have been a great deal more humane.

Helen was washing her hair when the phone rang and
she dived at it before it could wake Tansy.

'Miss Andrews?'

Ross Maclean's voice came over the line like a dark
spell and she gripped the phone tightly.

'Yes.'

'I called to say that I'll pick you up in the morning.
It's damned cold. Please be ready.'

'Thank you. My address is——'

'I know where you live. The file has your address—
that's where I got this number. Goodnight, Miss
Andrews.'

Curt. Curt to the point of rudeness. Still, there was
no love lost between them. She thought he was ruthless
and he thought she was no better than she should be.
Why he was taking her she couldn't think. She didn't
want to leave Tansy—heavens, she got little enough time
with her as it was—but this was one way she could make
sure that her job was an ongoing concern. She would

have to make quite sure that she shone at whatever it was she was supposed to shine at. She finished drying her hair and then snuggled down in bed. Outside it was blowing a gale, snow in the wind, not surprising at this time of the year. At least she would be picked up in a Mercedes.

It was still dark as Helen got ready the next morning. Tina stole out of bed to see her off, standing with a look of admiration as Helen finished dressing. She wore an oatmeal-coloured trouser suit, tight trousers tucked into knee-length boots of pale-coloured suede. It was very smart, exclusive-looking. She had braided her hair as usual but this time she had left it hanging down her back, a thick rope of blue-black, startling against the suit.

'Chic, very chic,' Tina observed, huddled in her dressing-gown. 'I've never seen it before.'

'I never did wear this,' Helen murmured ironically. 'The deal that this was supposed to bring off fell through before it even got started.'

There was still bitterness in her voice as she remembered the many ways that Miles had used her, and Tina's face darkened.

'Pig!' It was the only thing she ever called Miles and Helen relented as she saw her sister's face. Tina had suffered too.

'Sure you can manage?'

'Sure I'm sure,' Tina said, walking to the bedroom window and looking down as a car drew up outside. 'I say, I think he's here. Oops! He's getting out. Ten feet tall. Does that sound about right? He *looks* all right.'

'There's nothing all right about him,' Helen muttered, flinging a bright red cashmere shawl around her shoulders and picking up her weekend case. 'I'll phone when I know where this hotel is, then if anything goes wrong——'

'Nothing will go wrong,' Tina said hastily, pushing her to the door. 'Get going. He's not about to ring the bell, he's just standing leaning against the car, freezing no doubt.'

'Hmm! He certainly won't improve with the keeping, even refrigerated,' Helen observed tartly, but all the same she moved fast. She crammed a felt oatmeal-coloured hat on her head and made for the door.

She felt shaky inside. It was the first time she had ventured beyond the town since she had moved here after the divorce. She was uneasy, scared to leave Tansy, scared to step out into anything she did not know. Miles Gilford had taken all her confidence and it had been a long fight back. It was only now, as she prepared to travel with this hard, uncompromising man, to go to a city she did not know, to leave Tansy and Tina behind, that she realised she had not won the battle yet.

He straightened up as Helen opened the door and came down the path. He was in a dark suit, an expensive-looking sheepskin jacket open over it, but she didn't have the chance to inspect him closely. His eyes flashed over her swiftly, taking in very aspect of her appearance in a second. He opened the car door and settled her inside, taking her case and dropping it on to the back seat, and she felt crushed by the swift, all-encompassing glance. The dreadful urge came to her to ask if she would do, and she bit her lips together as he got in beside her and started the smooth, powerful engine.

For a while he said nothing, but as they sped on in smooth silence he glanced across at her.

'All right?' His quiet enquiry startled her and her eyes met his, blue and anxious.

'Yes.'

'Did you manage to make baby-sitting arrangements?'

'My sister lives with me.' She didn't feel like talking. Inside she felt sick. The car, for all its size, seemed to be enclosing her, pulling her close to him, to the male power of him. Her eyes seemed to be drawn to the tautness of his thighs, his leg nowhere near her but seeming very close. Fear welled up inside and she tried to breathe deeply, to shake it off. There was a nauseous feeling of being trapped.

'Are you afraid of flying?' She looked up at his soft question and he glanced across at her, a sidelong glance that made her sit up straight. He often looked like that, shooting a glance at her with shimmering grey eyes that seemed to strike at her nerve-endings.

'No. I haven't flown for some time but I used to.' When she could be useful to Miles.

'Then what are you afraid of—me?'

'You know I'm not.'

She was instantly on the defensive, her voice sharpened, and he drove in silence before he said, 'I know I'm supposed to think that, but sometimes I wonder.'

'Don't wonder about me, Mr Maclean,' Helen said shortly. She felt him stiffen instantly and regretted her sharp voice. After all, she was with him for a day and a half. It was pretty stupid to go on to the attack right away. 'Sometimes—sometimes I worry about home, that's all,' she finished quietly.

'I see. This sister—how old is she?' He seemed to relax and she breathed a sigh of relief.

'Nineteen. She's very responsible. She—she had a bad time when she was in her final years at school and now she takes evening classes to get more A-Levels. She's good at languages. Next year she'll go to university.'

'I see,' he murmured again. 'I understand your need to leave at five. And what happens to your arrangement when your sister goes away to university?'

'I haven't thought about that yet,' Helen confessed. 'No doubt something will come to me.'

'What happened to your parents?'

'They died—a car accident. My sister was fifteen.'

He nodded. 'So now you're the head of the family.'

'Yes.' She relapsed into silence, not quite sure how she had come to be telling him anything. One thing at least: the oppressive feeling of danger had drifted away, he didn't seem to be enclosing her any more. She wasn't sure how it had happened—maybe it was the dark sound of his voice. When he wasn't angry there was a velvet quality to it, as if it belonged to another person from the man she knew. She often hung on to the sound of his voice, remembering it afterwards.

When he parked the car the wind was wild, catching Helen's smart hat and blowing it into the air. He fielded it with one long arm and handed it back, his eyes amused as he saw her thick braid, vividly black against the bright red shawl.

'I'll take your case. You clutch the hat,' he suggested wryly and for a minute she was startled by the warmth in his eyes.

She didn't have much time to consider it though because the plane was ready straight away and they were airborne before she had time to think. She was grateful for a cup of tea and closed her eyes for a minute as Ross Maclean ordered a black coffee and then settled down to his papers. Slowly she relaxed, feeling almost light-headed. Tension had been building for two weeks and she had to try to relax out of it. She knew perfectly well how migraine could hit her. It was a miracle she had survived this long.

She took off her hat and after a while slept, totally unaware of the cold, hard eyes that glanced at her. The thick black braid had fallen over her shoulder, her lashes were curling against her smooth cheeks, dark and lustrous as the thick hair that framed her face. She was beautiful, innocent-looking, almost tragic as she rested back against the seat.

His lips tightened. How deceptive appearances were. He knew that from past experience. He turned away impatiently and his attention was instantly on his papers, his mind alert only to figures and ideas. It would amuse him to see Claude Thiriet's face when he met Miss Andrews. She looked so defenceless. He would ooze charm and she would freeze him icily.

CHAPTER THREE

IT WAS an impressive hotel, and it was also quite obvious that Ross Maclean was known here. Things seemed to go smoothly for him always, Helen noted almost absently. She wasn't used to that. She was quite accustomed to hotels like this, though; big impressive hotels that cost too much, Miles the worse for drink, his cruel fingers digging into her, his fierce mutters—'Smile! Smile! Smile!'

She had been the front for Miles so often as he'd struggled to project a wealthy image, an image he was certain would bring in business to a failing firm. She had dressed up carefully and smiled brilliantly at people, knowing that she would suffer for it later if she didn't. She was used to things going wrong, the bills that were more than he expected, always her fault, tightly suppressed anger in public until even the waiters knew. It was like stepping back in time, except that things didn't go wrong with Ross Maclean. *His* wealth and power were real, his easy authority bringing instant attention.

'Miss Andrews?'

He was looking at her curiously, waiting for her, the keys in his hand, and she pulled herself sharply to the present, following him to the lift, still feeling detached but quivering with nerves all the same.

'Do you feel all right?' He looked at her closely and she gripped her hands tightly together, meeting his gaze with enquiring eyes and a small, cool smile.

'Perfectly.' Her brisk voice had his eyes narrowing slightly and any momentary concern was instantly banished. He nodded curtly.

'As it's still early, we can get breakfast. I have a few things to do so I've ordered something in my room, I've also ordered for you. As there's no choice, I didn't consult you. A Continental breakfast doesn't leave much room for manoeuvre.'

'Thank you. I didn't eat before I left home.'

'I assumed as much.' He stopped by her door and handed her the small case. 'We have a meeting at lunchtime and another this afternoon. This evening is a social necessity. For now, though, you're free, although I would prefer it if you did not leave the hotel. I may have to get in touch with you.'

'I'll unpack and rest,' Helen promised, letting herself into her room and almost at once sinking to the bed.

She could hardly believe that the door was locked, that she had the key. So greatly had this trip brought back the past that she almost expected to see Miles striding in, see the cruelty in his eyes, hear him blaming her for his current failure. She shuddered and began to unpack. She wasn't sure if this was therapeutic or a torture, but she felt pretty secure that nothing would go wrong. Ross Maclean was across the wide corridor, his room almost opposite.

She glanced at herself in the mirror, amazement on her face. What was she thinking? Ross Maclean didn't make her feel secure, far from it. Since his arrival she had been more on edge than she had felt for all of two years. He represented about as much security as a tiger.

Helen changed into a soft, coffee-coloured dress for lunch. She had matching shoes and a thick chocolate-coloured belt enclosing her small waist. After a certain amount of consideration, she left her hair in the braid, hanging beyond her shoulders. With high heels it somehow added to her height and gave her confidence. She made up carefully, using her favourite perfume, something she never used at work where perfume seemed out of place.

She hadn't realised there would be two meetings during the day and she felt a trifle gleeful that at the last minute she had added another outfit to her case. She was making a point on the subject of clothes and she knew it. Maybe he would feel embarrassed at offering to buy her some? She doubted it though. He would probably be speculating about where she had acquired them. His opinion of her was all too clear.

He rang through and then called for her, his gaze going over her slowly as she opened the door. His eyes seemed to be smokily grey, softer than they had looked before, and for a minute she had a feeling of unaccustomed warmth, as if something gentle had touched her. Nothing gentle ever touched her, unless it was Tansy patting her face in a sleepy manner. The feeling held her transfixed, although he never smiled.

'A very disturbing housekeeper,' he murmured in a rather self-derisory tone. 'I apologise.'

Helen's face flushed softly and his lips tilted in the semblance of a smile then.

'Better and better. We'll go down before you undergo another startling change. Got your notebook?'

'Yes.'

'Of course,' he murmured wryly. 'What prompted me to ask, I wonder? I imagine that little bag is filled to the brim with office paraphernalia.'

'One notebook, one pencil,' Helen managed quietly. There was something about him that had put her off her stride, some subtle change in his manner, a warmth that made her feel vulnerable. She was suddenly intensely aware of him, an awareness she had never before felt with any man. It brought a haunting purple shadow to her eyes, a tingling to her skin as he took her arm.

She understood his change of attitude when she saw the guests they were entertaining to lunch—all men. Her heart sank and for a moment she stopped quite still. Remembrance came, nauseatingly sharp, the past whirling back again.

She was supposed to charm them. That was why he needed her. Why had she never thought of it? That was why he had been so insistent about clothes. History did repeat itself after all. His gentleness had been deliberate, to get her started. He was more subtle than Miles, naturally—he was more intelligent, and he couldn't beat her afterwards. She felt quite sick.

'For heaven sake, what's wrong with you?' he muttered as she stood transfixed. 'How many times do I have to ask before you tell me? If you're ill then say so now and I'll send you back to your room. I could manage without you at a pinch.'

'I'm not ill,' Helen said quietly, standing as straight as a rod. 'You don't have to manage without me, Mr Maclean. I'm quite used to this sort of thing.'

'A wide selection of men? Please don't enlighten me,' he snapped, his previous warmth gone instantly. 'Just do what you came to do; after all, it's part of your job.'

'Yes. I can see that now,' Helen murmured, turning her face away when he glanced down at her angrily. He didn't get the chance to make any other remark because his guests were waiting, at least two of them looking intently at Helen.

There were four men, three of them obviously from the Middle East, in spite of their lack of flowing robes. The fourth man was French, middle-aged but still handsome, and they all stood as Ross Maclean took her arm and led her to the bar. The introductions were swift and friendly and Helen hardly had the time to take in all the names before he was turning to her.

'My secretary, gentlemen.'

'Does she have a name?' Claude Thiriet looked at her with sleepy, sensuous eyes and Ross Maclean answered.

'Helen,' he said quietly.

Not that it should have surprised her. She wasn't likely to get much charming done if they had to call her Miss Andrews. They were to call her Helen and flirt with her. She was to respond and lull them into an attitude that would make it easy to get a contract signed. She was bitterly disappointed in him. He hadn't looked as if he needed this sort of thing, though perhaps all businessmen were the same. She was hardly experienced enough to know. Embarrassment and misery just engulfed her.

Settled to lunch, Helen found herself close to Ross Maclean, and after the soup talk turned to business. She had taken care to keep her eyes as much on her food as possible because it didn't take much intuition to fathom the looks she was getting from the Frenchman and from one of the other guests. It was a relief to hear figures being bandied about, products being discussed.

'Do you want me to take notes, Mr Maclean?' she asked hopefully, wishing she had big spectacles of a forbidding variety. So far she had given small wan smiles in the direction that was obviously expected, but she was finding it too hard to take and didn't know how she would face anything more that was needed.

'Whenever you think it necessary, Helen. I leave it to you. We'll sort things out later.' He sounded very impatient and no doubt she had said the wrong thing but she took out her notebook and pencil all the same and put them firmly on the table.

'Is this beautiful creature usually so formal or is this for our benefit?' Claude Thiriet asked. ' "Mr Maclean" sounds a little too cold to be true.'

He glanced at them suggestively and Ross Maclean's voice had an icy edge.

'Helen is the perfect secretary. I can't imagine managing without her.'

Helen tensed. She could tell from the hard voice that Ross Maclean was angry, that he had expected more from her than formality.

'Even though you are "Mr Maclean"? My secretary calls me *chéri*.'

'And what does your wife call you?' The icy edge was more pronounced but Claude simply shrugged.

'She calls me *chéri* also. I have a way with women.'

Helen smiled brilliantly even though her face threatened to stiffen and set like that, and Claude Thiriet's eyes looked more seductive than ever. She dared not glance anywhere else and she had little time after that. Ross Maclean conducted business at such a fast and furious rate that she hardly had time to eat.

After lunch the meeting broke up, arrangements being made to meet at four-thirty, and Helen trailed miserably after her hard-faced boss as he motioned her in the direction of the lift.

'Now we'll sort out all that before this afternoon swamps us.' He stopped outside his room, his glance disparaging as Helen hesitated nervously.

'You're perfectly safe, Miss Andrews,' he snapped. 'I have a suite, bedroom, bathroom and sitting-room. A girl with your social ability should have nothing to fear. You won't get any further than the sitting-room. We revert to formality now. I know you prefer it with me.'

She didn't reply and he motioned her inside his small but impressive suite, leaving her no time for nerves. She was here to work and work she did! He simply drove on like a dynamo, snapping out questions, dictating notes and keeping her so busy that she never raised her head.

'Right, that's about it,' he rasped later, glancing at his watch. 'Come downstairs at four and I'll be in the bar. I'll show you where we go from there.'

'Yes, Mr Maclean.' She felt greatly subdued, not entirely sure of her role, and he stopped her as she reached the door.

'Perhaps you could bring yourself to call me Ross?' he enquired caustically. 'After all, I believe it was Jim for your former boss. With Thiriet insisting on being called Claude I hardly like to remain so formal. I feel like a rather formidable stepfather of the Victorian era.'

'You—you want me to call you...?'

'Ross. Go on, say it. It won't bite.'

'Ross, then,' Helen murmured, her face flooding with colour.

'There!' he drawled sardonically. 'It's quite easy really. *Chéri* won't be necessary.'

'Or even remotely possible!' Helen snapped. She banged the door as she left, but she was in her own room with the door locked before he could do anything about that.

Helen didn't know quite what to do about the afternoon session. She seemed to have done everything wrong at lunchtime. One thing was sure, whatever she did he would be annoyed. She couldn't really understand why. It seemed to her fairly obvious that she had two functions here. So what was he so cross about? Maybe she should have acted more flirtatiously right from the first? The trouble was, she couldn't. She had never been able to do that sort of thing. Miles had told her she was a frigid little bitch, unable to respond to any man, not even capable of pretending it. No doubt Ross Maclean thought similar things.

She was surprised to find him reasonably affable when she went down again at four. After much thought she had decided to change in view of the fact that she had brought the clothes with her. She wore a wrap-over dress in red jersey. Maybe he would think she was overdoing it a bit, or maybe he would think she was being insolent after his remarks about clothes. She couldn't win anyway, so what was the point of trying?

He was in the bar by himself, and he stood and came towards her when she stopped hesitantly in the entrance.

'We'll not linger here. I imagine you're more interested in tea than a drink in the bar?'

'Yes, please.' She felt quite flustered by his change of mood, his sudden half-smile.

'Yes, please, Ross,' he insisted, taking her arm and swinging her about. 'We'll work our way into that before the others arrive.'

They went through to the coffee lounge and he ordered tea for both of them.

'Bring *mademoiselle* a few sandwiches,' he added as the waiter left. He glanced at her. 'As you ate very little lunch you can nibble a few sandwiches now. Have you phoned home?'

'Yes. I telephoned this morning. I—I tend to get a bit anxious when I'm not within calling distance.'

Helen looked around the lounge, disturbed by his intent gaze and trying very hard to avoid it. Now was the time really when she should ask him outright exactly how she wanted her to behave. She had tried both ways and neither seemed to please. He appeared to have got over his annoyance and to be giving her another chance— or at least getting her back into the right mood, she hastily corrected. She should ask him now, but unfortunately her nerve wasn't quite up to it.

'Have you always lived where you live now?' He was studying her averted face, her pure profile, and his eyes remained intent and probing as she turned.

'No. We lived in Hampshire, a very small village. We moved, though, after...'

She stopped as she realised she had been going to tell him about the divorce. It could have been quite spectacular if she had pressed her advantages, but she had only wanted to get away, to free herself of the fear, the humiliation, quickly. The village where they had lived had been too small for her to lose herself in the crowds— there were no crowds. She wondered if Miles was still there? He probably still had the same grand house, one he could not afford. She had infuriated her solicitor by refusing to claim anything. All she had wanted was freedom and safety.

'After you had the baby?' Ross frowned across at her, looking as if he was trying to reckon her up, probably imagining she had fled in shame.

'No. Before then.'

'You must have been very young—twenty-one? You're not much more than a girl now. It looks pretty obvious without your office disguise. At the moment you don't look capable of managing such a burden.'

'She's no burden!' Instantly Helen became angry, defensive, and he looked at her impatiently.

'I didn't mean your daughter. I meant your position as head of the family. Eat your sandwiches, Helen. Maybe if I keep quiet we'll get through the rest of the day amicably.'

'I'm sorry. I'm a bit touchy on the subject.'

He just nodded uninterestedly, turning his attention to his tea, and when the others came in they were sitting in silence, his attempts at conversation ended.

The afternoon meeting was more formal, a room having been put at their disposal, and this time Ross pulled no punches. He was here for results and expected them. A package was worked out, dates fixed, prices discussed, and as they rose to leave it was clear he had taken a firm grip on their minds and whirled them along. There was a faint air of exasperation about him, a take-it-or-leave-it attitude that surprised Helen.

'*Mon Dieu,* he gets worse,' Claude Thiriet murmured as they strolled out into the foyer. He took Helen's hand, tucking it under his arm, and short of wrenching herself free she could do nothing. 'I have seen him in New York and he is much the same but without this cold edge. Perhaps it is you, my dear Helen? In America the lady with him was extremely attentive. Is it possible that you are not giving him what he needs?'

'I work for him.'

'So did she, as far as I could tell, but she was obviously offering more than office skills. She was very—affable.'

He looked at her sideways, his glance almost openly explicit, and Helen cringed inside. How often had she had to put up with this? She blushed. She couldn't help it but it seemed to delight Claude.

'I have it now. You are a little tease. This evening you may tease me.'

He took her hand, kissing it with a flourish, and she looked up into cold grey eyes as Ross came across to them.

'You can stop your act now, *mon ami,*' he said impatiently. 'Helen has her notes to transcribe.'

'It is no act, Ross. Helen and I have just been planning our night.' He smiled and walked off and so did Helen.

She couldn't work out the expression on Ross Maclean's face. It might have been approval or disgust. She was suddenly beyond caring.

Even so, when she was placed close beside Ross at dinner, she felt pleased. It gave her some sort of status, a feeling of safety, but it did not last long. There was no way of getting out of dancing with each of them. It seemed to be expected, and Helen cursed the defiant attitude that had made her bring a dress with a low back. Their fingers seemed to be drawn to it, first the Middle East Romeo and then Claude Thiriet. She tried to ignore it and keep on smiling but inside she was almost sick, a slow fury kept down by her very bad memories. It almost seemed that she was programmed in how to cope with this sort of situation. Miles had trained her well, more with the stick than the carrot.

When the evening ended she didn't wait for Ross. She nodded a hasty goodnight and went off by herself, tossing down her bag when she was safely in her room and looking with disgust at the dress, her eyes hot with unshed tears. She knew she would burn the dress as soon as she got home—her skin seemed to be crawling with loathing.

A knock at her door startled her, anger and fear beginning as she thought of Claude's satisfied face as she had left. If it was him . . . The knock came again and then a hard voice she was beginning to hear in her sleep.

'Helen! Let me in!'

When she opened the door he strode inside with no explanation whatever and turned to face her, slamming the door behind him. She had infuriated him, that much was plain.

'What the hell was that all about?' His eyes drilled into her, hard chips of glittering ice. 'You're supposed

to be my secretary, not some vamp. If you've arranged
to entertain Thiriet here later you can just——!'

'How dare you?' Helen stared at him as if he were
mad, her face flushed with annoyance. 'Am I responsible for your lecherous clients? You arranged this! What
did I do wrong, or are they into something I haven't
learned? They wanted me to beat them with my
handbag?'

He looked about to shake her. 'I wanted you to behave
in a decent manner. I didn't expect to find you giving
the "come on" to Thiriet and gang.' His lips had a white
line of temper around them and Helen's face paled at
his next words. 'You're a real myste , aren't you? All
cool at home and all seduction at play. You intend to
continue the evening in here? It's a nice big bed.'

She lashed out at him, catching him off guard, her
fingers leaving a red line across his cheek, and his head
snapped back but only for a second. His eyes narrowed
to icy lights and he came forward grimly, rage on his
face as Helen backed away, feeling the hard edge of the
dressing-table against her legs.

'Don't touch me! Don't touch me!' She had gone
chalk-white, her blue eyes enormous, filled with terror,
and it stopped him in his tracks as if he had met a brick
wall.

'I don't strike women, Miss Andrews,' he grated.
'There are other methods of punishment.'

It was quite clear what he meant and she cringed away.
'No! I'd rather you hit me. I couldn't bear it.' Her voice
rose, her hands tightly clenched together, and he stopped
again. He looked stunned, shocked out of rage.

'Are you out of your mind? You've been pawed all
evening. What sort of a performance is this? Every one
of those damned men was running his hands over you.

Am I to be excluded? Don't I get a brilliant smile if I touch you?'

'Stop it! You wanted me to smile.' Helen's face went whiter than ever. 'I didn't have to be told. I'm used to it. It's what I always had to do and I tried my best because I need this job, but now I—I can't do it any more. I can't come with you again. You'll have to bring somebody else who can be like that because I can't and I won't and...'

Her voice rose, hysteria at the back of it, tears springing to her eyes, and he sat down slowly, never taking his eyes from her.

'I think you'd better explain,' he said quietly.

'There's nothing to explain. I've told you.' Her voice sounded raw but he just looked at her steadily.

'I think there is. You've just accused me of using you to procure business, unless I'm mistaken. Let me tell you, Miss Andrews, that I don't need that sort of assistance. Our products are the best and they sell. We have a list of clients lined up and waiting impatiently. The only reason I drive hard at things is because I can't bear to waste my time tiptoeing around. When the time comes that I need a beautiful face to move products, I'll sell out my shares and take to the hills.'

'Then why—why did you bring me?' Helen whispered. 'Why did you tell me to get dressed for Paris?' Her voice choked but she got no sympathy—if anything he looked angrier than ever.

'I told you to dress for Paris because Paris is where we are,' he rasped. 'You know damned well why I brought you, you're my secretary!'

Helen stood watching him, tears like small drops of rain on her cheeks, sliding down the pale creamy skin in a stream of misery.

'I—I'm sorry. I—I misunderstood. I thought that ... I'm sorry.'

There were more tears now, embarrassment adding to her misery, but he made no sign of relenting, his voice was no less harsh.

'Sorry is not going to do at all. You've not only made me look like a bloody fool, you've made me into a scoundrel. Sorry doesn't cover that lot. I want an explanation.'

Helen dared not look at him. She stood there wringing her hands together, not even daring to wipe the tears from her face. She had misunderstood him because she was still not free of the past. She had made herself look cheap.

'Sit down, Helen.' His voice had lost a little of the cold emphasis and she sank to the dressing-stool, her legs trembling. 'Now. Talk!'

There was no way she was going to get out of this and no way she could meet those clear grey eyes.

'It was when I was married. You—you think I'm an unmarried mother, I know, but I was married when ... Miles had a business, not successful, he was always in debt, but he had big ideas. He was determined to succeed but he never did. From the first I was supposed to—to lure clients. These clothes... I had to—to smile and smile to put up with——'

'Why the hell didn't you refuse?' His interruption sounded enraged and she looked up at him then, meeting his furious eyes and cringing more at such raw savagery.

'Unlike you, he believed in striking women, and I couldn't just walk away. I was too scared and—and there was Tina.'

'Tina?'

'My sister. She lived with us. She was only fifteen. That's partly why I allowed myself to be rushed into

marriage. When my parents were killed Miles was wonderful and—and I believed him. I thought it was love.
Everything was just too much and he was kind... Tina
was so young.'

'And you were so grown-up, all of twenty. My God!
Tonight you thought I wanted you to do the same thing
all over again?'

Helen nodded, looking down at her feet, too shattered
to face him.

'Oh, thank you, Helen,' he said caustically. 'I can see
you've really got me reckoned up. If I had too much
pride, you've certainly punctured it.'

'I'm sorry,' Helen said wearily. 'I'm well programmed, you see. It was all so familiar.'

She looked up and he was staring at her, his mouth
tight, and she looked rapidly away.

'I feel dirty.'

Her voice was a whisper and he just went on staring
at her. It was more than obvious that if he offered any
comfort she would either scream or faint. His black scowl
was enough to unnerve her.

'Get a shower.' He got up and brought her silky robe
from the bed, handing it to her carefully, his voice a low
growl of anger. 'I'll order you a tray of tea for when
you come out.'

She was too subdued to argue and when she came
back, securely wrapped in her robe, he was still there,
the tray of tea on the small table beside him.

'Sit down and drink your tea and you can pour me
one, although I feel in need of something stronger.'

She was almost frighteningly obedient and he sat
watching her, his eyes on her bent head, her shining hair,
blue-black in the lamplight. Her slender hands were still
trembling. She looked beaten, defeated, no sign of his
efficient secretary left.

'How did anyone manage to get you so intimidated?' he bit out suddenly. 'You're intelligent, capable, beautiful!'

'In the quiet privacy of a house, might is very often right,' Helen told him without looking up. 'I was still shattered from losing my parents, feeling terribly responsible for Tina. I suppose it was easy for Miles. I fell into a great big trap and he started straight away. He worked up to better things. I never came out of the shock of one thing before another shock was there. I was scared, bewildered, prepared to believe I was everything he said.'

'What made you finally leave?'

She gave a peculiar little laugh. 'He went too far.'

'How?'

'Please don't ask me.' She suddenly looked up, her face still pale, a dazed look in her eyes. Her voice was back to a whisper. 'Do you know, I can't think now why I didn't kill him.'

For a second he looked back at her, his narrowed eyes trying to probe her mind, and then he looked away, leaving her in peace, his face flaring with anger as his gaze fell on the silky blue dress she had worn that evening.

Before she knew his intentions he had got up and walked over to it, picking it up and tearing it straight down the middle.

'If you want it replacing, just say so,' he grated as she stared at him in astonishment, his violent action bringing her out of her odd trance. 'In fact, if you want your whole wardrobe replacing let me know.' His lips suddenly twisted wryly at her expression. 'At least it's given you something to think about besides my lecherous clients.' He strode to the door. 'Go to bed, Helen. Let's hope your next trip to Paris is an improvement on this one. In the morning we'll get the hell out of here early.'

He walked out without saying goodnight and she was so worn out by tension that she just climbed into bed and closed her eyes. Oddly enough, it was a relief that he knew. She had seen a great deal of savage satisfaction on his face as he had ripped the dress in two and thrown it into the waste basket. It had satisfied her too, as if she were rid of those pawing hands. She drifted into sleep, light-headed and weary, an angry, handsome face with piercing grey eyes uppermost in her mind.

Next day their departure could not be early after all. The airport was fog-bound and it was late afternoon before they were cleared for take-off. Ross was grim-faced, almost completely silent. He was very courteous, seeing that she was comfortable, arranging for them to stay a few hours extra at the hotel, but underneath she could feel his displeasure. She could almost hear him thinking and she felt a complete failure. She hadn't forgotten that he had told her she had made him look a fool. This excursion had brought back too many bad memories and she was quiet and pale, her face almost drawn. That didn't please him either.

By the time she got home it was dark. Ross just walked to the door with her case, put it down and nodded to her politely, and she went inside feeling as if she had been severely chastised. Tansy was in bed and, when Tina rushed from the sitting-room to ask excitedly about Paris, Helen just brushed past her and went upstairs.

'Well, how was it?' Tina appeared at her bedroom door and stood watching her quizzically.

'It was awful!' Helen burst into tears. She didn't explain further because she was too upset, and a migraine started, the worst she had ever had.

CHAPTER FOUR

IT WAS about ten o'clock the next morning when the phone rang and disturbed Helen. It prompted her to wonder vaguely if Tina had phoned the office but she was really too ill to care. Tina seemed to be shouting but she couldn't hear properly from upstairs and she drifted off again with Tina's voice ringing in her ears. She hardly seemed to have slept at all when the doorbell rang and her disturbed sleep became an impossibility as Tina began to shout again, a sort of subdued ferocity about her voice that told Helen she was really annoyed.

She struggled out of bed and into her thick dressing-gown, wrapping it tightly around her, and Tina's voice grew in volume as she opened the bedroom door.

'If you think you're coming here to upset her some more then you can think again! She wouldn't be in the state she's in if you weren't so awful! She never had a migraine when Jim Saxton was there, so don't try to wriggle out of it!'

Helen clung to the rail and went slowly down until she could see the door. It was wide open, cold flooding in, Ross Maclean standing on the step in driving snow with no hope of entry. Tina was guarding the door like a dangerous terrier, her dark hair bobbing about with annoyance as she shouted. Tansy was hiding by the kitchen door and Ross was looking astonished.

'Tina!' Helen's voice was weak and she couldn't really see properly, her vision badly affected. She swayed dangerously and Tina rushed at her, grabbing her arms, almost unbalancing her.

'Tina, for heaven's sake!'

'What are you doing up? Sit on the stairs while I see to things and then I'll get you back to bed. Go into the kitchen, pet, where it's warm,' she added to Tansy who was biting her nails anxiously. 'You stay where you are!' she added loudly as Ross made a step forward.

Helen looked over her sister's head at him. He was only a blur but she could see his amazed face. He couldn't be laughing, could he? Of course not. This was where she got the sack.

'Look, I'm sorry. I—I have a migraine and——'

'Go back to bed. Don't bother about him.' Tina tried to lift her and the whole situation became fraught with danger.

Ross Maclean strode in and took over.

'Call off the dog.' He picked Helen up as if she weighed nothing at all. 'Where's bed?'

'First door at the top,' Tina snapped. 'But you needn't think that——!'

'Oh, Tina, please!' Helen muttered and Ross glanced at Tina's furious face.

'Seconded, Tina,' he remarked, climbing the stairs steadily, his burden effortlessly held to his chest. He looked down at Helen. 'Next time, give me the password, please. I know a lot more about myself than I did this morning, all of it detrimental. I may never get out of this place alive.'

'She's quick-tempered,' Helen murmured, pain keeping her eyes closed.

'She needs a licence. She probably bites.'

Tina was right behind them, bristling at his sarcasm. 'You can put her on the bed. I'll see to her. She needs a tablet.'

'Right.' He put Helen down and regarded Tina with mocking interest. 'I enjoy being useful. May I get your muzzle now?'

'Listen you, you're not *my* boss!'

'Tina, please stop. None of this is really his fault.'

'You could have fooled me!' Tina's voice changed like magic. 'Oh, what are you doing up here, pet? Mummy has a very bad head and——'

'Now it's worse,' Ross put in, smiling down at the tiny figure who held on to the door.

'Is it a fight?' Tansy was all blue-eyed worry and he walked across to pick her up right before Tina's outraged eyes.

'No. It was just shouting.'

'Tina can shout,' Tansy offered solemnly, her little arm going trustingly round his neck.

'She probably has a medal for it. What's your name?'

'Tansy.' She looked at him with the interested, steady gaze of a child. 'It's a weed,' she volunteered.

'It's a wild flower,' Tina snapped, trying to help Helen into bed.

'It's a herb,' Ross corrected firmly, looking at Tansy. 'It has bright yellow flowers, very pretty, like you.'

'Flattery will get you nowhere,' Tina muttered darkly, pulling the sheets to Helen's neck, and Ross grinned at her, not at all annoyed apparently.

'It's doing well so far. She hasn't shouted yet.'

'That's because she doesn't know the whole story,' Tina began, ready to strike up again, but Helen interrupted wearily.

'Look, my head is killing me. Can you go and fight somewhere else?'

'Me too?' Ross looked across at her, his silvery eyes taunting.

'If you must.' There was a peculiar expression on his face and she closed her eyes quickly, her defence mechanism alerted as usual.

Tina snatched Tansy away from him very possessively and made for the door.

'I'll get you a tablet, Helen,' she said, glancing at Ross Maclean pointedly, but he was not at all put out. He walked over to the bed as Tina snorted with rage and went down the stairs.

'You've painted a very black picture of me,' he said quietly. 'I got one instalment on the phone when I rang earlier and your sister continued the narrative when I arrived to see how you were. She called me a domineering brute. I have to object.'

'She didn't hear the latest happenings,' Helen murmured, even her own voice hurting. 'I'll bring her up to date when I can get up.'

'How often do you get like this?'

'Not for a while. Not in the last two years—well, not this bad.'

'Then it probably is my fault after all. Maybe I am a domineering brute.'

'I expect I asked for it. I made a complete fool of myself in Paris and, anyway, I deliberately let you think I was an unmarried mother.'

'Why?'

'I don't know. Defiance perhaps. I suppose I just hate men—well, most of them.'

'Dear me. I'll have to work on that.'

Helen looked up at the sound of his voice, so quiet, his eyes faintly amused. Maybe he was fuming inside. She didn't know him, after all. He was tough, self-possessed and she could never see beyond the barrier of those crystal-clear eyes.

'I'm sorry about Tina. She's very protective. How are you managing at the office?' Her voice seemed to have gone husky and his eyes narrowed slightly.

'Fairly well. Jeanette is playing at being you. You can straighten out all the mess she's made when you come back. I'd better go before that sister of yours creeps up behind me with a heavy instrument.' He paused at the door. 'Don't hurry back. Get well.'

Helen listened for more trouble but apparently he got out safely and she was just settling again when Tina came up with her tablet and a drink.

'So that's the Maclean of Maclean's,' she mused. 'Isn't he gorgeous?'

Helen squinted up at her, swallowing the tablet with difficulty. 'You *roared* at him!'

'Well, he deserved it, but those wonderful eyes have a very nice twinkle. I could fall for him.'

'If you were older and quite mad,' Helen muttered, settling down to sleep. His eyes did have a twinkle, she realised. He was strong too. He had carried her so easily and she hadn't cringed once. It was odd really, she seemed to be still hearing his voice.

Helen felt a lot better next morning but Tina persuaded her to stay in bed. It wasn't really restful. In the first place, Tansy was all over her, climbing on the bed and playing in the room. It cut deeply at Helen. Tansy saw very little of her really; only the weekends were free for playing and going out. It worried her but she couldn't think of a way round it. She was the head of this small family, the bread-winner. In the second place the phone rang several times and Tina was bounding upstairs to ask for information. The office seemed to be in turmoil.

'Ross wants to know where the Swiss file is.'

'Filed under "S", for heaven's sake. What on earth is Jeanette doing? I'm going to be run off my feet straightening things out when I get back. Ross?' she added in surprised enquiry as Tina made for the door.

'Well, he *did* insist. We've worked out our differences.'

'Wonderful!' Helen noted Tina's flushed face, a nagging worry growing. Ross was a very handsome man, the sort of man that any young girl might find irresistible. There was also a sort of aggressive sexuality about him that for herself was frightening, but for Tina it might be exciting. The sooner she got back to work and cut off all lines of communication between them, the better.

Helen went back on Wednesday, taking everyone by surprise. It was half-past eight and Jeanette had not arrived. Naturally, Ross was there, walking into her office when he heard movement and standing looking at her with unfathomable eyes.

'Are you really recovered?' She was still very pale, the whiteness of her skin a sharp contrast with the blue-sheened black hair.

'Near enough.' She looked apprehensive, avoiding his eyes, and he gave a small laugh, low in his throat, almost a sound of triumph that crackled along her nerve-endings like an invisible current. She looked up warily, surprised by his smile.

'Couldn't wait to get back?' he asked softly. 'Well, I can't say that the sight of you displeases me. Get your feet firmly under the desk before Jeanette gets here. She's running amok.'

'Maybe I made a bad choice?' Helen asked quietly, sure he would think so. He surprised her.

'No. It was a good choice, she'll fit in when you've got her trained. At the moment though she's swamped, and she doesn't have your intelligence, nor your experience—after all,' he added drily, 'she's very young, only twenty-three.'

It was slightly taunting but it was said with a smile and Helen managed a smile of her own, a weak one only. She was on unsafe ground with Ross, almost breathless for some reason, a chemical reaction she could not control.

'I'm sure she'll age.'

'With me? She's bound to. In fact she aged a great deal yesterday. You'll find things a bit chaotic. When we move upstairs it's going to be worse until we're sorted out. We'll be ready after Christmas.'

Helen took off her coat and straightened her suit jacket a little self-consciously. He wasn't making any move to go back to his own office and she noticed his eyes lingering on her hair. It was still braided and hanging down her back.

'Any chance of your staying tonight?' he asked almost absently, his voice curious as if he was thinking about something else.

'Yes. It's Wednesday. Tina doesn't have a class tonight—in fact the classes have closed until mid-January, but . . .'

'I know. I won't make a habit of it. You need time with Tansy and I expect Tina could do with a break. I thought tonight we could catch up on some of the sorting out, because things are still piling up.'

Helen nodded and turned to the mail, dismissing him in the only way she knew how. He was disturbing her. He had always disturbed her but now he was closer somehow as if she had allowed him to step near. She didn't like it but it was only natural, she supposed. He *had* carried her up to bed, after all. She blushed painfully and unexpectedly, looking up to find him still there, his eyes intent on her flushed face. He didn't say anything but his glance was half amused, and she remembered she had once felt he could read her mind. She hoped he couldn't.

She met the day head-on, already moving like a whirlwind before Jeanette had even arrived, and it took no time at all for her assistant to get the message and settle to hard work. Ross was wryly amused, his eyes meeting hers as if they had planned it together. It was almost secretive and she was stunned at the pleasure it gave her.

Tina was busy cooking when Helen rang to say she would be late.

'I'm not surprised. Ross said your new assistant was barely coping. I think he had a bad two days when you were off.'

'You're very knowledgeable,' Helen observed crisply. 'Did you shout information to each other during the fight?'

'Well, I had to apologise before he went and he stayed for coffee. Tansy really took to him.'

'Where was I when all this social activity was under way?' Helen asked, feeling worried.

'Out cold with your tablet. I don't think he wanted to go back to the office at all really. I did wonder actually if you were thinking of inviting him home for a meal tonight. He's still living in a hotel, you know.'

'I'm definitely not thinking of it,' Helen assured her firmly, her blood running cold. Tina was interested in him after all. It was a complication she could do without. Tina was nineteen and Ross was a sensual man, dynamic—dangerous.

'Well, please yourself, but I'll put some extra food on just in case. Goodbye, chief.'

Tina rang off and Helen stood looking at the phone as if it were about to leap up and bite her. She was trying to think back to being nineteen. How had she felt? Gullible. One word said it. Except that there had been her parents, her father's steady guidance. Even so, it hadn't stopped her from rushing headlong down the path he had warned against once he was gone.

That was different though. Miles had seemed to be a safe anchorage. She hadn't wondered about loving him really. If things had been different she would probably have waited and got to know him better, found him out. As it was he had pressurised her and she had folded easily, the responsibility of Tina like a weight on her heart. Loving had never entered into it. She had been stupidly naïve, only finding out the hard way what life offered. Tina must not drift into that, but Helen had no real idea what to do.

She was still worrying and working at six-thirty when Ross called a halt.

'That's enough, Helen. I'm tired out,' he announced standing in her doorway. He looked tired too. She had never seen him look even remotely weary before, but there seemed to be lines of strain around his face that she couldn't fail to see.

'I didn't think you could tire. I imagined you were automatic.'

The words just came out without thought and she flushed with embarrassment as soon as they had left her tongue. He laughed, though, the sound bubbling up in his throat.

'Insult or praise? I'm not sure how to take that.'

'I'm not sure why I said it. I don't normally make personal remarks.'

'You don't normally make remarks at all.' He was watching her closely and she was even more flustered.

'Well, Jim Saxton said you were a human dynamo. I think he was a bit scared of you.'

'Are you? Scared of me, I mean?'

She stiffened, recognising all over again that he was dangerous—being tired didn't make him safe. He was a man greatly to be avoided; all men were. She didn't answer and he sighed, his hand massaging the back of his neck.

'I must admit that I don't usually feel so jaded. It probably has something to do with hotel living. I'll have to get around to finding a house. There just hasn't seemed to be a minute to fit that in though.'

'Are you going to buy one?' Helen looked up at him in surprise, her shyness momentarily squashed.

'I think so. I've got a whole sheaf of information from estate agents, but I've only seen one that interested me and that not enough to stir me into action.'

'But—but you'll have to sell it again when you go back to New York.' Now why did that worry her?

'Possibly.' He dismissed the subject handing her her coat and reaching for his. 'Well, back to the White Bear. Let's see, Wednesday. It's quiche and salad—they're nothing if not predictable.'

He didn't have much choice either. The White Bear was the only decent hotel within driving distance of the offices. Her eyes slid to the windows. The snow hadn't settled but it was still there, coming down as sleet now, cold and unfriendly. Treacherously her mind pointed out how amusedly kind he had been when she had her migraine, how angry he had been in Paris and how his actions had made her feel better.

'Would you like to have dinner with us tonight?' The impulsive words were out before she could stop them and he seemed to be rooted to the spot.

'Invite me again, slowly and calmly,' he ordered, his eyes intent on her flushed face. 'Please be careful what you say.'

'I—I thought you might like to have dinner with us tonight because it's so cold. Salad and quiche don't seem to be suitable on a night like this.'

He was watching her closely, seriously, a smile growing slowly along his lips. 'Thank you. I'd like to. Are you sure you can cope with one more hungry person?'

'There won't be much to do. Tina's been off all day and she doesn't have to go out tonight. I expect everything will be ready. She—she likes cooking.'

'She's a little powerhouse. Do you like cooking?'

'Yes. When I have the time. I used to...'

Her voice trailed away and she looked resolutely out at the snowy night. Why on earth had she done this? He was as male as they could get, filled with everything she hated and feared: masculine aggression, sexual power, unbending strength. Just because he had looked tired...

'Don't freeze up on me, Helen. It's cold enough outside as it is.'

His quiet words dragged her back to the present and she met rueful eyes.

'Want to back out of this invitation?'

Why, oh, why could he read her every action so well?

'Of course not. I wouldn't have suggested it if I hadn't meant it.'

They were fencing like two duellists but Helen knew her own inexperience. She was backed into a corner and she had brought it all on herself.

In the dark warmth and luxury of the car Helen began to regret her impulsive gesture even more. She almost felt as if she had been willed into doing it, either by Tina or Ross himself. For the greater part of the day she had been dwelling on the necessity of keeping Tina as far away from him as possible and now she was hurtling home, taking him with her as a guest. She hadn't even phoned to let Tina know. Suppose everything was a mess? Tina cooked very extravagantly, using every utensil she could lay hands on, her efforts sometimes left lying on any table in the house. There would be Tansy's toys all over. She was too het up to talk all the way back.

Inviting warmth and the delicious smile of cooking met them as they stepped into the little hall and Tina poked her head around the kitchen door, her eyes filled with laughter as she saw them together.

'Hi, chief! Hi, Ross!'

He was smiling broadly and Helen wondered where his natural hardness had gone. Tansy flew at her and Helen hugged her close, burying her face in the soft curls.

'I ate,' Tansy assured her. 'I had a bath too. Can I stay up a bit?'

'Yes, you can, chicken,' Helen agreed, thinking hastily of safety in numbers. 'I'll just help Tina.' Really, she was about the worst hostess in the world. Ross was still standing there.

'All is prepared. Just go and get changed, no business suits at dinner.'

'Can you find me a caftan?' Ross enquired and Tina grinned at him, in no way overawed by his very masculine presence.

'You'll do. You can go and pour a drink while I dish up. You can also entertain Tansy. See if the fire wants tending,' she called over her shoulder as he took off his coat.

'These are my teddy-bear pyjamas,' Tansy pointed out, coming to stand close to him, and Ross bent to inspect them.

'They're very smart. I might get some myself.'

Helen fled upstairs, realising that her hands were shaking. There was an easygoing way between all of them as if she had missed something. They really seemed to know each other and in such a short time. It was ridiculous but she felt left out, as if Ross Maclean had breached the walls of her fortress in some sinister way. Having invited him here of her own volition, she now felt as if she had been outmanoeuvred.

She put on a soft blue woollen dress, a shade darker than her eyes, standing brushing out her hair without really thinking about it. Tina's face had been flushed with more than the heat of the kitchen, her eyes too bright. This was going to lead to trouble. She clipped on her earrings and went downstairs, quite prepared to find Ross in the kitchen talking to Tina. He wasn't. He was in the sitting-room with Tansy, a drink in his hand, and Helen felt like running out when he just stared at her.

The light caught the shining jet of her hair, picking up the blue lights, and the intensity of his gaze made her skin burn. She realised she hadn't re-braided her hair because she didn't bother at home. It made her feel vulnerable and unprepared.

'Incredible,' he murmured. 'Another outer shell removed. You look younger than Tina.'

'I—I'll go and help her...' Helen began but he came forward and handed her a drink.

'I have orders to keep you here and I'm trying to remain in her good books. I've entertained Tansy, tended the fire and poured you a drink. If I've missed anything out, she'll snap, so stay here and defend me.'

Helen sat down, and Tansy immediately climbed on her lap, cuddling against her.

'Can we make a snowman?'

'Not until the snow gets deep,' Helen reminded her, kissing the tip of the little nose. 'We might get a sledge this year,' she added, and received a hug that nearly spilled her drink.

Ross was still watching intently and she struggled to find a safe topic of conversation. 'What sort of house will you be buying?'

'Something old and fairly big. It will have to be used to entertain, unfortunately.'

'Why unfortunately?'

'Because this sort of house would suit me a lot better. It's cosy and warm, easy to live in.'

'You should have seen it when we got it! It's only an old cottage really. We could afford a modern kitchen and a good bathroom; the rest is—improvisation. We don't even have a dining-room,' she added, nodding towards the cosy alcove that housed the dining-room furniture.

'Who needs one? I can't think of anything better than eating dinner with a fire blazing in the hearth. I've lived in great houses all my life.' He grimaced. 'My mother entertains a lot, business and personal preference. I don't remember being allowed to stay up and have a cuddle while guests were having cocktails. Anyway, this place is full of antiques by the look of it.'

'My father collected them,' Helen said, her eyes on the flickering flames of the fire. 'We have some of them here and the rest are in store. We couldn't bear to part with them, each piece was important with a little story of its own, even if it was only how my father tricked the dealers who were bidding.' She smiled as memory flooded back, the firelight making her skin gleam like cream silk. She shook herself out of it, looking down at Tansy. 'You're sleepy. Want to go to bed?'

'No! I can sit at the table, Tina promised.'

'I did too. Come and get it!' Tina appeared through the door that led from the kitchen to the dining area and Helen saw that she had nipped up to change. Her dark brown hair was brushed and shining and she was in a short woollen dress that showed off her long legs. She was wearing make-up too, a thing she usually didn't bother about. A chill seemed to settle on Helen but she managed a smile and kept it there as they all sat down to eat.

Tina had made a great effort. The table looked wonderful, the dark, polished wood gleaming in the lamplight, the main lights switched off, candles lit, flickering shadows on the old silver.

'Ooh, lovely! We don't get out candles much.' Tansy gave the game away but Tina was totally unmoved.

'Well, I thought we wouldn't eat out of the pans tonight as we have a guest,' she said briskly, dishing up the meal competently as Tansy climbed on to Helen's knee and watched wide-eyed.

'I could eat this out of a pan any day,' Ross complimented, highly amused by Tina's quips.

'Why, thank you, sir. You should taste Helen's cooking, though, that really is *something*!'

'Will I get the chance?' His disturbing grey eyes rested lightly on Helen but Tina was in full swing.

'Not unless you give her the day off. It's too late to start cooking at this hour. She cooks at the weekend though. You could come then.'

Helen looked dumbfounded and Ross smiled his slow smile. He could see rejection of the idea on her face because she didn't have time to hide it.

'We'd better see how I behave this time, don't you think?'

He looked at Tansy, who was regarding him with open admiration. Helen was having trouble eating around her but she didn't want to ask her to get down. Tansy needed these moments.

'Come and sit with me,' Ross suggested, smiling into the watching blue eyes. 'I'll share indigestion with

Mummy.' Tansy instantly jumped down and he lifted her on to his lap, settling her against him, eating with no difficulty.

She was asleep before they had even finished the first course and Tina came to pick her up and carry her to bed.

'A visit here is fraught with danger,' Helen observed, sipping her wine.

'I know. I never back down from a challenge, though.'

She looked up quickly, her eyes startlingly beautiful in the light of the candles, a warning thrill running over her skin. What did he mean? Was he determined to be involved with Tina or was there something else? She couldn't look away, her ability to hide her face deserting her. Power held her fast, only Tina's re-entry breaking the sudden spell; even so, the slight smile seemed to hang around his lips for the rest of the evening. When he had gone, the house seemed quite, quite empty, and as they washed up together Tina was unusually silent. She looked smug too, excited. Helen hardly dared to think about this, the possible consequence of her impulsive action.

There was a lull in the bad weather the next day. Overnight rain had cleared the snow completely and the sun was shining, doing its best against a cold, clear sky. Ross went out to lunch with a client and Helen had the office to herself for a while as Jeanette lived close enough to be able to have lunch at home. Helen normally brought a packed lunch and now she ate it slowly, her eyes still on her work.

Ross had been quite right about things piling up. She was still eating and working when he came back in.

'That's a really good way to relax,' he said sharply, his tone making Helen hastily pack away the remains of her snack. 'Where's Jeanette?'

'She'll be here in a second.' Helen glanced at her watch, relieved to hear Jeanette's high heels tapping across the passage right then.

'Good. Get your coat. We're going out.' He glanced at her impatiently when she still sat there. 'Now, Helen!'

'Right.' She jumped up, reaching for her coat and bag. 'Do I need my notebook?'

'No.' He ignored her for a minute. His attention taken up with Jeanette. 'Get these typed, Jeanette, and then get to some of Helen's work. We'll be out for about two hours. Note any calls and we'll discuss any problems later.'

He swept Helen out of the office with the same impatience and Jeanette raised shapely eyebrows at Helen. Now what? He seemed disgruntled but Helen couldn't think of a thing she had done wrong. She decided to ask no questions, even when he drove out of town and headed into the country. It was safest in her little fortress of silence and she had been in it for so long that sliding back into it was not difficult.

'Don't you have any sort of normal curiosity?' he suddenly snapped as they were speeding along the nearby motorway. 'Do you ever think about more than your notebook and pencil?' His sudden wave of anger was startling and Helen looked at him in astonishment.

'Often!' She was stung into a sharp reply. 'Why, I even ponder on world events from time to time. The washing drives me wild with excitement and as to shopping...!'

He gave a soft laugh, flashing her a glance of amused admiration. 'I can see, Miss Andrews, that you've stopped being afraid of me.'

'I never was,' Helen muttered quickly, using the low, bright sunlight as an excuse to hide her face.

'No?' He snapped down the sun-visor, taking her excuse away. 'Then you'll not lose your nerve when I tell you that I'm taking you to see a house, a lonely, empty house.'

'Why?' She shot him a look of acute anxiety which he noted with amusement.

'Aha! Terror returns. To put your mind at rest and satisfy your well-concealed curiosity, I'm thinking of buying. I need your advice.'

'Oh!' Helen relaxed a little and then looked at him curiously. 'Why me?'

'Why not you? Women have a way of seeing faults. I might be overwhelmed by its attractions and never see the rising damp.'

'If you're set on an afternoon's entertainment, then be my guest,' Helen snapped, feeling uneasy about this teasing, an unhappy trembling disturbing her inside. She didn't want to be alone with Ross, miles from anywhere. The idea upset her, although she couldn't think why.

'Just walk round and look,' he suggested quietly. 'I won't ask you to entertain me in any way at all.'

There was sufficient innuendo for Helen to feel her cheeks burning, and she had not in any way recovered when he said,

'How long are you going to go on being scared of men, Helen?'

'I'm not scared of men. I was only ever scared of one man. As to the male species, I don't like them.'

'That's unnatural. You're very young and very beautiful. You don't seem to have been scared of Jim Saxton,' he added before she could blush.

'Jim was different.'

'He presented no challenge. He let you sink into your little office and hide away. He was too intent on having an easy time to bother you. His golf handicap was paramount.'

'Oh! How do you...?'

'I know just about everything that concerns the firm,' he murmured sardonically, leaving the motorway and heading across country. 'Don't start worrying about Saxton. He was too good to throw away and too lazy to leave here. He'll jump in New York, snap out of his lethargy. When are you going to snap out of your nightmare?'

'I just work for Maclean's,' Helen said stiffly. 'I'm not lethargic and I don't need saving by you or anyone else, so don't probe into my private life, Mr Maclean.'

'How would you like to be dumped out here in the middle of nowhere?' he asked coolly. 'You refuse help and yet you don't seem to me to be very good at survival. Maybe you need a sharp, hard shock!'

'I've had one. *You* arrived!' Helen snapped. It seemed to her that he had deliberately started this nasty quarrel and although she had improved a lot lately, especially with having to deal with Ross Maclean, she still trembled at the thought of an open row. 'If you want to try your experiment then I suggest you stop here and drop me off,' she finished in a choking voice.

'A few hundred yards,' he murmured. 'Then you can get out and run.'

Helen turned her face away, looking out of the window, her heart taking on a wild hammering when he drew up smoothly by a tall hedge, the country road empty around them.

'You can get out now,' he said evenly, and Helen could hardly believe it. He actually meant it. He was about to leave her here miles from anywhere. She tightened her lips and opened the door, not quite knowing what to do. If he thought she was going to beg he could think again. She set off.

CHAPTER FIVE

'WRONG way, Helen.' Ross was beside her in two strides, his hand tightening round her wrist when she tried to pull away.

'I can choose my own way,' she managed chokingly, but he merely turned her and took her along with him.

'The house is here. Surely you're going to look at it now we've come?'

'I suppose you think that was damned funny, telling me you were going to tip me out?' She planted her feet firmly and looked up at him angrily. 'Or do I get tipped out on the way back?'

'What a child you are really,' he said softly, his eyes grey and intent on her flushed face. 'Fright builds a wall around you. What man in his right mind would dump you miles from anywhere?'

Suddenly, tears flooded into her eyes, tears she blinked away rapidly.

'Miles was in his right mind, but he dumped me out once. It was dark, cold and there was nobody——'

'Damn! Damn! Damn!' He used his grip on her wrist to pull her forward, looking down at her in wild exasperation. 'That's twice I've walked into a situation without warning. How the hell was I to know that your damned ex had behaved like a lunatic outside the house?'

'He wasn't a lunatic,' Helen said quietly, looking down at her feet. 'He was just a cold, unfeeling man.'

'You're wrapping me up in the same parcel?' he asked with dangerous quiet.

'Not quite,' she said softly. 'For instance, I know you don't hit women and now I know you don't dump them alone on a country road.'

'But I'm also a very undesirable male animal.' His voice was flat, edged with anger, and she didn't look up.

'I've given you my opinion of men, and then only because you've—you've pressed me for details. If you'd left me to get on with my work like Jim did then I wouldn't have said a thing to deflate your ego.'

'Thank you,' he murmured drily. 'In other words I'm responsible for my own injuries? Let's get on with what we came to do, Helen, and then you can get back to your tidy desk and your safe little way of life.'

He was too angry to speak again and she walked along beside him, a mixture of misery and resentment flooding around inside her. She hadn't asked him into her life. She hadn't asked him to probe into her mental attitudes. He was her boss and nothing more than that. Now he was furious because his chauvinistic joke had gone wrong and, typically, he was blaming her.

When he took a key from his pocket she came to herself and looked at her surroundings. The house was a Georgian house of quite a good size, red brick, its well-balanced proportions pleasing. It stood in a lot of garden with old red brick walls around the outer perimeter. There were mature trees in about two acres, gardens that looked as if they had been neglected for only a short time, and in spite of her anger and unease she found her eyes roaming over it slowly and with a great deal of pleasure.

'If you'd like to look around I'll be grateful for any comments,' he said stiffly as he let her into a wide, well-lit hall.

It was hardly a promising way to begin but she didn't want to talk to him anyway and she started on her own, going upstairs first as he was obviously about to go round the downstairs. The more she saw of it, the more it grew on her. It was a lovely house, and by the time she came to look around the lower floors her annoyance had faded to a sort of wistful nostalgia.

Her own home had been like this, not as large perhaps but very similar. Even the rooms were arranged in the same way and she could see the furniture they had so carefully kept, the pieces in store, her mind placing them unerringly as they had been in the days when there were no worries, no heartaches, when she and Tina had seemed to laugh each day away.

She came slowly down the stairs almost visualising her mother, arranging flowers in the shining hall. Her blue eyes clouded. It was gone, all gone, the memory of Miles and what he had made her see in herself too much in the front of her mind for her to be able to hang on to the happiness.

She walked through into the lounge, so sure of her steps, so lost in the past still that the sudden appearance of a change of level about a foot from the door took her completely by surprise. There had been no such step in her own home and she pitched forward headlong.

Strong arms caught her and she looked up into clear grey eyes as Ross held her firmly and looked down into her face. She was so taken aback that she made no sort of move to free herself.

'That step didn't used to be here.' Only as she said it did she realise how odd it sounded.

'Didn't used to be here? You know this house?'

'No.' She shook her head impatiently, her impatience with herself. 'That was a stupid thing to say. What I meant was that this house is almost exactly like my own home, the one that Tina and I grew up in, and I've been so much back in the past that I thought...I mean, I didn't expect...'

He looked stunned, his grip on her tightening.

'Are you telling me that I've done it again? You'll no doubt think it was deliberate. Maybe you imagine I'm some sort of professional torturer?'

'I don't imagine anything of the sort,' Helen assured him quietly. 'I was lost in the past and I just didn't expect any changes at all. There never was this step at home. I was just remembering how my mother used to fill the hall with flowers and...' Tears suddenly flooded her eyes. 'It was so safe, you see. I just stepped right back into it. It was all before... You were right after all,' she choked, 'I am a child—daydreaming.'

'I didn't mean that at all,' he said almost angrily, his hands tightening. 'When I said you were a child I meant your impossible innocence. It's almost unreal to think that Tansy belongs to you, that you've been married. I don't see anything of it in your face—no experience at all.'

'It's there,' Helen said quietly, blinking the tears back and turning away. 'What you see is not innocence, it's coldness. I told you—I don't like men.'

'I'm not *men*! I'm me!' He swung her back, his hands on her shoulders, his angry insistence taking her by surprise. 'How the hell am I going to stop hurting you if you don't give me a clue? How many more traps am I going to walk into?'

'None at all,' Helen managed coolly, his hands on her shoulders beginning to worry her badly, an uneasy excitement starting inside. It was quiet in the house, not a sound for miles and miles but their own voices, and he was angrily reproaching her for something that had been outside her control. 'Just leave me alone.'

For a minute he stared down at her in wild frustration and then, without warning, he pulled her totally into his arms.

'I'll leave you alone when I'm good and ready!' he grated, his arms tightened to a crushing grip, his grey eyes flickering with icy fire.

Helen struggled then, a wave of panic washing through her, but he bent his dark head and caught her mouth with his before she could do more than make a small sound of protest and she seemed to be stung with fire. Faintness washed over her, panic mixing with a very forbidden pleasure that she had never felt before. She had a mental picture of Miles, his mouth hard and wet grinding into her, and she was fighting before she realised that this was not the same.

Flames licked at her, taking her breath away, puzzled anxiety asking her odd questions. He was not in any way cruel but there was an insistence that demanded subjugation. He was the master, dominant, taming wild fears. His hand cupped her head, forcing her into closer acceptance of his mouth, his probing tongue between her lips bringing a spasmodic and wild reaction as it penetrated deeper.

Dazed and shaking, she was completely subdued, incapable of any struggle now, her body guilty of an unfamiliar melting as he crushed her closer, his mouth languorous, moving against hers with complete mastery. She had never felt this before, this actual, physical ache, this inability to move, her body sleepily heavy with something she didn't understand. She had suffered the physical attention that Miles had forced on her but now she seemed to have given up all attempts to save herself, allowing Ross to ravage her mouth and force her into an intimate embrace that shocked her.

Dimly she realised she was kissing him back, her arms tightly around his neck, an empty hunger in her that needed assuagement. For another second he let the hunger continue, fuelling it with lips that burned her, and then he made a low sound of protest, easing his mouth away slowly.

When he lifted his head she stayed right where she was, trembling too much to move away, only upright because he held her so. His thumb probed her cheek, almost gently, the grey eyes brilliantly clear.

'Please let me go.' Her eyes were no longer blue but deeply purple, locked with his.

'Are you sure?'

His voice held the edge of irony and his softly taunting attitude quickly dispelled the hazy cloud she had floated on, shame coming quickly to take its place.

'I'm perfectly sure. I think I've had enough of your experiments, Mr Maclean!'

'Don't be a fool, Helen!' he rasped, suddenly angered. 'If that was an experiment it was a very dangerous one in this empty house and you've got a very low opinion of yourself. I kissed you because it's the natural reaction when a very beautiful girl is in my arms and I stopped because my next natural reaction would have been to take things a good deal further.'

'I didn't ask to be in your arms,' Helen hissed, anger rising to cover her growing feeling of shame at her own complicity and the entirely unacceptable feeling of loss now that his lips were not over hers.

'No. You just fell into them,' he taunted softly. 'You don't look quite so full of hatred for the male of the species any more either.'

'I learned the hard way to disguise my feelings,' Helen snapped, pulling free, shivers running over her.

'Did you?' he mocked softly. 'You would be a credit to the acting profession. Your body language was explicit, you melted right into me, your lips opened like rose petals.'

'You forced me!'

'I held you,' he agreed, 'but there was no force, Helen, and you know it, even if you can't admit it. You wanted to be right where you were.' He suddenly smiled. 'It was the reaction of a completely innocent girl, one who has never known a lover.'

'You think Tansy came from under a gooseberry bush?' Helen muttered turning her flushed face away, taking an uneven step to the door.

'I'd rather not think about how Tansy came into being,' he grated, angry with such speed that she shuddered. 'Dwelling on that might just provoke me to murder.' He took her arm in a completely impersonal grip. 'Let's go!'

'The experiment is over?' She turned at the open door of the house as he found the key and looked at him with what she hoped was distaste. He paused, his eyes steadily holding hers, not allowing her to look away now when she would have liked to.

'Obviously,' he said quietly. 'To complete the experiment I would have had to take you to bed. The idea was beginning to drift to the top of my mind.'

'Stop it! I hate the way you talk! I hate your damned assurance that you only have to crook a finger to get anything and anyone. Don't be so certain that there's so much difference between you and Miles Gilford either. You've both got the same soaring male ego. You even taste the same!'

She was so angry, so afraid of her own reaction to him, so humiliated by his quiet taunting that she never thought of his reaction to such words. It was only when she saw violent rage staring at her through icy eyes that she stopped, her face red and angry, her hands shaking.

'Just be thankful that you saved that until you were back in the cold air of the outside,' he said through clenched teeth, his eyes drilling into her like chips of ice. 'You like to live on the very edge of the world, don't you? Make the mistake of talking to me like that when we're alone indoors and you'll really learn how I taste and I won't have to ask you about your secrets, I'll know every one of them!'

Helen turned and ran down the path but he was right behind her, grasping her wrist when she would have passed the car and run along the lane alone.

'Let me go!' This time she fought wildly but he simply opened the door and bundled her inside.

'No way. I'm not about to let that frozen little mind put me safely into a category. I don't leave women stranded. If you want to get away from me, Helen, all you have to do is resign.'

'And obviously I will.' She huddled in the corner, her face turned away. 'I can't stay at the office now, not after this.'

'After what?' He started the car and backed out into the road, not even looking at her. 'Let's see. You have to resign because I kissed you and you responded like a normal woman. Or is it because you felt the need to hit out at your own feminine response, to hide your feelings by saying unforgivable things to me?'

'They weren't unforgivable,' Helen muttered heatedly, drowning in humiliation, hating him.

'They must have been, because I don't forgive you.'

'Then of course I'll resign.'

'You're a free agent,' he said coldly. 'Do whatever you wish.'

On the way home, Helen still trembled. She had been shocked out of her frozen state by kisses and hard, warm arms and her reaction had been wild, over the top, childish. It was that last that stung most of all. Any normal woman would have laughed and come back to the office with her grace and dignity intact. Instead Helen had huddled in the corner of the car like a child, hiding from both Ross and her own aching reaction to his kiss.

Oh, what a mess! Why hadn't he simply left her alone? Did he have to try his skill on every woman he saw? He had even managed to make Tina into a dithering teenager when normally she was swift and competent, a mirror image of all Helen herself had been.

She was afraid that her day's experience would show on her face, and she still felt dizzily adrift, not quite earthbound, as she walked slowly up the path to her own front door. It was wrenched open, Tina almost pulling her inside, and Helen's own problems were forgotten as she saw Tina's face white as a sheet and scared, so scared.

'Tina! What is it? What's the matter? Tansy...!'

'No. She's fine.' Tina looked at her for a minute and then pulled her towards the sitting-room. 'Come in here, Helen. I've put Tansy to bed... She's perfectly all right but I had to get her up there out of the way. I promised I'd send you up later and she could come down but...' Tina ran a hand through her hair, her face frantic. 'I— I haven't made any dinner. We'll have to have beans on toast or something. I fed Tansy——'

'Tina! Stop this now! Tell me what's wrong before I go mad.'

Helen grabbed her sister's arms and gave her a little shake. To tell the truth her own legs were feeling weak because this was not Tina at all. Something had happened and it had been bad. Anything less than awful would have had Tina in a rage, throwing plates.

'He came,' Tina said in a whisper, sinking to the settee. 'Pig came. He wants Tansy.'

'Miles? Miles was here?' Helen's voice was just an unbelieving croak and Tina looked up at her through eyes that she now saw had been weeping copiously.

'He came just after lunch. Helen, where were you? I've been trying to get in touch with you all afternoon!'

'I went out with Ross. He dropped me off at the bus on the way back.' While Ross had been holding her, kissing her, while she had been responding like a mindless fool, Miles had been here, getting Tina into this state. 'What do you mean, he wants Tansy?' she demanded, coming out of her trance of disbelief. 'He doesn't stand a chance. We were divorced even before Tansy was born. A couple more months and he wouldn't even have known she existed.'

'He does know, though, Helen, and he wants her. He says he has as much right as you to her because he's her father. He says he's marrying again in a month's time and he'll be able to offer her a home better than this and a wife who doesn't have to go to work and leave her with a teenager. He's taking it to court as soon as he's married.'

Helen sat down, her face as pale as Tina's. 'Did Tansy see him?'

'No. He wanted to come in but I kept him at the door. It made him madder than ever but I wasn't letting him inside.'

'Thank goodness!' Helen frowned, puzzled as well as scared. No court would hand Tansy over to a man who had never even seen her, father or not. 'He can't do it. He's bluffing, only trying to start trouble. How did he know where to find us anyway?' she suddenly asked.

'The vicar's wife. Don't you remember she sent on some things for us, the things that were at the cleaner's?'

Tina looked at her in miserable reproof and then burst into tears. 'Oh, Helen, why did you just go away quietly? Why didn't you fight for anything you could get, then this wouldn't be happening? The court would know how he treated you. It would all have come out. They wouldn't let Tansy go to such a violent person.'

'They won't now,' Helen said through lips that were stiff with fear. 'He has no rights whatsoever.' Would they, though? Did he have rights? Uncertainty welled up inside, choking her.

'They won't know now!' Tina sobbed. 'It's all too late. How will you fight this? How will you prove after all this time that he was a brute and frightened us so much? They'll ask why you didn't bring it to court, why you had an amicable divorce. That's what you allowed him to tell everyone—you were getting an amicable divorce.'

It was true. In her anxiety to get away she would have agreed to anything. She had been afraid for Tina, for herself and for the baby not yet born. She had agreed to keep silent for a very speedy divorce. The court battle she had dreaded was now being forced on her.

Suddenly, Helen couldn't sit still any more. She jumped up, pacing about. Did he have the right? The law was so strange, so convoluted, sometimes justice seemed to have very little to do with it. Miles was Tansy's father, wanting to offer her a home. He wouldn't win, she was sure of that, but to what extent would *she* lose? The very least they would do was give him equal visiting rights and how could she face that, knowing that Tansy was with someone as vile as Miles, even for one day? She might have to let her stay the night, a weekend even. In fact, he might win. She had no idea. Tansy would be in court, so would Tina. Everything she had fought to hide would be out in the open, sordid and cruel.

She ran upstairs, creeping into Tansy's room, leaning over her. She was so precious, this sleeping child, her curly black hair against the white pillow. The thought of Miles even touching her at all sent waves of cold fear through Helen. She turned and went down the stairs, walking into the kitchen where Tina was making a tray of tea.

'We'll leave. We'll move,' she said determinedly. 'He may be playing another cruel game but I'm not risking it. I'm not risking the law either. Tansy is not going to be taken into any courtroom and neither are you. Tomorrow we'll start planning our move and act on it.'

'Suppose he comes while you're at work?' Tina asked, her face no less worried by Helen's announcement.

'I'm not going anywhere,' Helen said bleakly. 'I'll have to resign in any case because we're leaving and going a long way off. I may as well resign now. Morning will do.'

'What will Ross say?'

'Who the hell cares?' Helen snapped. Wasn't Ross another man, another dominating man, another cruel man? Let him cope with Jeanette!

They sat and talked until the early hours, both of them so anxious that they took it in turns to go and look at Tansy's sleeping form, the sight of her reassuring for a while. After only a few hours' sleep they were both up again, and at eight-thirty Helen shut herself in her bedroom and telephoned the office. It was Ross.

'I'm leaving today,' Helen said with no preamble as soon as she heard his voice. 'I know it's not normal to just walk out but I can't give you any time at all. I have to leave as from this moment and I'll let you have a written resignation in today's post.'

She put the phone down straight away, only just hearing his startled and angry exclamation as he rasped out her name, and then she pushed him out of her mind, trying to unscramble the thoughts she had brooded over during the long night. She had to sell this house without leaving a forwarding address. That could all be done through the solicitor, she was sure. They would need another house though right away and clearly it would have to be rented at first. Luckily there was a lot of rented property on the market at the moment and she only hoped that there would be an equal amount in the district they had decided upon.

They had an old aunt in Reading—they would move there. It was a place they knew. Miles knew nothing about her aunt, though, and this time there would be no forwarding address left for anyone, vicar's wife or not. She began to walk round the house, to plan their move, and after a hasty breakfast of nothing more than toast she started again. Tina was worn out this morning; tears and lack of sleep had turned her into something unrecognisable, and only determination kept Helen on her feet.

It was half an hour later that the bell rang and Tina was instantly afraid.

'It's him. He's come back!'

Her attitude sent a wave of fear through Helen but she squashed it flat. Fear was contagious, like a disease. She was no longer afraid of Miles. She was going to fight for Tansy in any way she could and right now she would very much like to have the chance to kill Miles as he stood at the door.

She stormed out and wrenched the door open, her furious eyes blinking in surprise when she found an equally furious face looking back at her as Ross stood on the step and glared.

'What's all this resigning rubbish?' he grated. 'I've never heard such bloody nonsense in my life!'

'I'm leaving,' Helen managed quietly, her heart not yet settled back into place from her determination to strike Miles down at her feet.

'I kissed you and you're leaving? Am I hearing things right? Look, I'll build a plastic bubble with a letter-box. You can sit in there and push letters out to me. I'll shout dictation to you through the hole, I'll even get you a two-way phone. Don't be such an idiot, Helen!'

'It's not that. It's——'

Tina burst into the hall as she heard them, her face still blotchy from last night's weeping, her eyes puffy and red, and Ross looked from one to the other in astonishment.

'What the hell's going on here?' he grated.

It was no use, Helen could see that. He looked about as movable as a tank.

'I think you'd better come in,' she said unevenly and he glared at her even more, stepping inside and closing the door.

'And I think you'd better start explaining.' He looked intently at Helen as she led the way into the sitting-room, not at all bothered that it looked untidy. She had even smoked last night, a thing she hadn't done for years.

Tina crouched up on the settee looking as if she had been beaten, and Ross looked at Helen as if it were all her fault. It was Tina who explained.

'Pig came,' she said shakily. 'He came yesterday afternoon and I couldn't get in touch with Helen because you were out of the office. He wants Tansy.'

'Start again,' Ross rasped, his brows drawn together in an exasperated frown. 'You lost me with the first word.'

'Pig wants Tansy!' Tina said in a subdued shout and Helen waved her to silence.

'Miles came yesterday,' she said quietly. 'He told Tina that he wants Tansy. He's getting married again in a month's time and he's applying to the court for custody. He seems to imagine he'll get it with a wife at home all the time. He won't but he might very well get visiting rights. I can't even bear to think of it, so we're leaving. We're going somewhere where he'll not find us and, if he does, we'll move again.'

'I see.' Ross took off his coat and flung it on to a chair. He sat down and looked at Helen evenly. 'You plan to run and never stop, I take it?'

'I can't risk anything. He may very well win. Whoever knows what a court will decide?'

He just nodded thoughtfully and looked at Tina.

'Any coffee for a shocked visitor?' he asked with a smile.

'Sure. I can just about manage that. I'd better see why Tansy isn't up yet anyway.'

She trailed out of the room, shutting the door, none of her exuberance left at all, and Ross turned grimly to Helen.

'I assume she knows all about Gilford's violence?'

'She does,' Helen told him quietly, looking bitterly into the fire.

'Did she also suffer at his hands?'

'No. He didn't get around to Tina. At first she didn't know but after a while he didn't care about that, just so long as nobody else knew. That's why he might win visiting rights. I was so desperate to get away, to get a divorce, that I agreed to an amicable arrangement. To the rest of the world, butter wouldn't melt in his mouth; we were incompatible but still friends.' She shuddered. 'Perhaps I should have killed him.'

'Stop talking like that! The chances are he'll be wasting his time going to court.'

'And chances are he won't. You don't know Miles. He's syrupy sweet, so persuasive. He'll come up with a story that will have them reaching for their handkerchiefs.'

'And they'll look at you and Tina and call you both teenagers,' Ross murmured thoughtfully.

'Thank you. That's a big help,' Helen snapped, beginning to pace about. 'It's not going to come to that anyway. I'm leaving. If I have to move weekly for the rest of my life he'll not get the opportunity to even see Tansy!'

'Have you seen a solicitor?' Ross sounded coldly practical and Helen glared at him.

'No! I'm not going to either. There's going to be no court battle for Tansy and Tina to face. My inclination is to run and that's what I'm doing.'

Ross didn't reply because the door opened and Tansy came in, clutching a battered teddy-bear.

'I slept a long time,' she observed, running to Helen, who picked her up and hugged her fiercely. 'Tina looks funny. She's got red eyes.'

'It's a cold,' Helen said quickly. 'I think I've got it too. Let's get you some breakfast.' She looked across at Ross, not quite knowing what to say, but he was standing and reaching for his coat.

'I'll have to go. I have things to do that can't wait—cancel my coffee.'

Helen nodded. He would have things to do. She couldn't think why the sight of him had given her a small burst of hope, as if he would come up with some fool-proof scheme to get them out of this mess. He was a man, going about his affairs, only angered because he was about to lose a secretary who had coped with the mountains of work he had flung at her.

'I'll be back at eleven,' he added, to her surprise. 'I'm taking you out to lunch—all of you. Meanwhile, don't answer the door. If the expression in your eyes when you opened the door to me is anything to go by, then the door is best left locked. I might have difficulty bailing you out if you batter Gilford to the ground on your own doorstep.'

'Our problems are not yours,' Helen said quietly, her face flushed at his easy ability to define her intentions. 'We really don't have time to go out for lunch anyway. I have to start telephoning and packing.'

'I don't think there's going to be any necessity to pack,' he murmured, his lips twisting wryly, 'not at this stage anyway. I suggest you relax, calm down and get ready for lunch. As to your problems not being mine, I'm making them mine.'

'But why?' She just stared at him, Tansy clutched to her breast.

'I have my own reasons. I'll tell you later when you're not on the edge of hostility.'

He walked out and Helen watched him drive away. She was in something of a dilemma. She didn't want Ross interfering with her life. All the same, it had seemed safe while he was here. She sighed and frowned thoughtfully. She was always having to remind herself that he was not safe at all, that he was a man, a man who made Miles look like a spiteful, cruel boy. She could deal with Miles herself easily now if he hadn't had this hold on her, the possibility of his being able in some way to claim Tansy. She shuddered at the violence she had felt in herself when she had thought he was at the door. No wonder Ross had seen it on her face.

It seemed to Helen that lunch with Ross was merely an exercise in how to deal with two hysterical females, a manoeuvre to calm them down. It succeeded with

Tina—she was almost eating out of his hand. Helen could have done without it. She had too much to do, too many things to prepare, and she was restless and edgy all through lunch and on the way back.

He showed no signs of leaving and he was gentle with Tina to the point of tenderness.

'Why don't you go and lie down?' he asked. 'You look as if you haven't slept all night.'

Neither had Helen but he made no mention of that and, in all fairness, Tina had faced Miles and had all afternoon yesterday to worry about it.

'I don't think so,' Tina said after a quick look at Helen. 'There's Tansy, for one thing.'

'I'm here,' Helen said a little sharply. What was the matter with Tina? She had never behaved like this before. She was giving the impression that Tansy was her own personal burden.

'Well, I think I'll take Tansy for a stroll anyway. She hasn't been out of the house for two days. You'll want to talk to Ross.'

'I don't need to talk to anyone,' Helen said firmly, giving Tina a warning look, but it had no effect. 'It's beginning to snow again.'

'We'll wrap up warm.' Short of ordering Tina to stay put there was little Helen could do and as she left, a very excited Tansy clutching her hand, Helen was forced to look at Ross. He was making her feel uncomfortable, making her feel peculiar in fact, his eyes burning into her.

'Would you like some tea?'

'No, Helen. I would not like tea, coffee or anything else. What I do want is for you to sit down, look at me and listen.'

'There's no way you can help, if that's what you're thinking. And why should you help anyway? Just because you'll have to find another secretary there's no need to go to all these lengths. Secretaries are ten a penny and——'

'Will you stop babbling on for just two minutes and listen to me?' he asked forcefully, his tone making her sink to a chair. 'So far, the only length I've gone to is to take your small brood to lunch. If you continue like this then I'll still be waiting to speak to you when they come back.'

'When they come back?' Startled blue eyes watched his implacable face. 'Is that why you wanted Tina to go and rest? What can you possibly say that Tina can't hear, and in any case——?'

'Helen!' He raised his voice, positively glaring at her, leaving her with her mouth open, words hanging on the end of her tongue.

'That's better,' he growled when she subsided into silence. 'Now. I want to go over the things that are driving you away from your house and your job. You assume that Gilford will, at the very least, get visiting rights to Tansy. He's going to present a case where he will be able to offer more than you can, including a wife who doesn't need to work, who can give all her time to Tansy. Whether he will win or not I do not know, but I can think of a way to stop him, right in his tracks before he makes any sort of application at all.'

'How?' She sat up straight and looked at him very earnestly.

'Knock the ladder right out from under his feet. He's getting married in a month's time. Marry me.'

CHAPTER SIX

FOR a minute Helen thought she hadn't heard Ross properly. She just stared at him, her eyes turning from bright blue to purple, colour leaving her face.

'What did you say?' She just whispered the words and he looked at her in exasperation, his lips tightening.

'You heard me, Helen. I'm asking you to marry me, and don't go into your usual frantic reaction.'

'You must surely be mad!' She jumped to her feet, feeling definitely unsafe when he got slowly to his feet too, filling the room, towering over her. 'If that's the way you go about keeping your secretaries then——'

'Oh, I'll need a new secretary,' he murmured. 'I don't want a working wife, and in any case we have to put up our ace to Gilford's queen. You stay home and look after Tansy. You become Helen Maclean, wealthy, secure and quite capable of taking care of your own daughter. He won't even try for custody and if he does—well, I pack a lot of punch in certain places. Not with the law,' he added as her eyes opened wider, 'in the business world, and he *is* in the business world, isn't he?'

Ross sounded softly sinister, like a prowling jungle cat, his astonishing eyes narrowed to icy lights, leaping at her and pinning her as they had done when she had first seen him.

'Well?' he asked as she just went on staring at him mutely. 'Are you going to think about it?'

'I don't have to think about it,' Helen managed stiffly, trembling inside. 'I have no intention whatever of marrying again. You know my opinion of men. One man in a lifetime is one too many as far as I'm concerned.'

'I had gathered that,' he said drily. 'I'm not proposing marriage for any other reason than mutual protection. You need help right now and I'm going to need help before very long.'

'You?' She looked at him as if he were truly mad. 'Since when has someone like you needed help?'

'Sit down, for heaven's sake,' he muttered, sitting himself when she sank back to her seat. 'Why the hell do you think I'm in England in the first place and why do you imagine I want to buy a house here and settle where my father's roots are? I was sent to school here to please him, hence my very English accent. Now he wants to have his roots more firmly fixed here than ever. He wants me to stay here, build the business up over here so that he can eventually come back himself. He also wants me to marry. My mother picked her out for her polish and background: a glamorous American heiress who's been pushed under my nose since she was about sixteen.'

'You—you're not telling me that a man like you would tamely——?'

'I'm glad you realise I'm not tame!' he snapped. 'However, I'm sick and tired of being manoeuvred, I'm bored with constant accidental meetings, carefully planned parties. I aim to get them off my back once and for all. I want to marry you, to take on Tansy and Tina, to have my own home and do a little settling down.'

Helen was silent for a long time and he just let her sit there quietly. In fact she was running the whole idea past her mind like a computer. She would be safe with Ross, as far as being physically safe went. He had been ready to protect her in Paris and even yesterday at the house he had not pushed his advantage when he had had her at his mercy. Could she bear to be with him, though?

Her skin shivered when she realised that she could. If she could relax with him a little more, get to know him better, she had the feeling that he would be a good friend, more than that. Tina and Tansy liked him. That brought her mind back to her recent thoughts. Tina had a crush on him. Still, it didn't matter after all because she could never let any man...

'It's very kind of you but it's out of the question.'

He looked explosive. 'I just told you that it is mutual protection. Believe me, I'm not being kind. I'm grasping opportunity with both hands.' He suddenly looked at her with narrowed eyes. 'Or is that the whole problem? You're afraid that I'll grasp you with both hands?'

'I've been married. I know what being married means, thank you,' Helen muttered, her face red. 'I still haven't got over the disgust.'

'I'm offering to protect you, to take care of all of you. In return I want a wife as a good cover, to protect me too. I want a hostess to see to the comfort of business contacts and I think I've made it quite plain that I don't expect any "luring" from you. As to us, you can have your own room and I will not come into it.'

'You're a man,' Helen pointed out in embarrassment.

'How nicely you put it,' Ross said caustically. 'Luckily I don't need you to boost my self-esteem. I am capable of controlling my base instincts and this would be a marriage of convenience, mutual convenience. I would feel no shame whatever in seeking female company.'

'I can see that,' Helen snapped. 'You have a reputation to keep up.'

'I'm glad you realise it,' he pointed out, his eyes burning angrily. 'Now what do you say to my proposal?'

'No,' Helen said firmly. 'I want my own house and my own privacy and it needs to extend to more than a bedroom. Thank you for asking me but I'm afraid you'll have to get your mutual protection elsewhere.'

'Very well, I'll go, but don't put the idea too far at the back of your mind.' He stood and looked down at her steadily. 'You may not get the chance to run too far and it's not much of a life you're planning. Even if you don't care for yourself, you could give some thought to Tansy, not to mention Tina. There's a long time to consider and perhaps a lot of running in it. You'll be traceable when Tansy is at school. What do you do then, uproot her and move, leave all her friends behind? Does Tina continue to run with you or do you finally scuttle off alone, dragging Tansy along?'

'Shut up!' Helen jumped to her feet and faced him angrily, not liking the picture he painted. 'You're making me into some sort of criminal, or lunatic. I didn't wish Miles into existence and I didn't ask to live my life with him in fear.'

'You had Tansy.'

'Yes. I had Tansy.' Her face was white, her eyes almost black with emotion. 'But then, you wouldn't want to know about that.'

For a second he faced her, his eyes burning holes into her mind, and then he turned abruptly away.

'No. It's none of my business, even less as we're not going to see each other again. I accept your resignation, Helen. Goodbye.' He let himself out and Helen was still sitting staring at nothing when Tina came back in.

'What did he say?'

Helen looked up at her in surprise. 'What do you mean, what did he say?'

'He wanted us out of the way to talk to you. I'm not stupid, Helen.' She looked disappointed. 'Don't tell me you just sat there and drank coffee.'

'He asked me to marry him.' Helen said it flatly and openly. If Tina had any ideas about Ross Maclean then this was a good way of putting paid to that. Leaving the district would help too.

'Great!' Tina let out a whoop of delight. 'Saved! I knew he wouldn't let me down, gorgeous man.'

Helen's face mirrored her shock. 'You're pleased? I thought you had a crush on him!'

'*Me*? I'm nineteen! Ross is one beautiful man but he's all of thirty-eight or even more. I made him welcome, that's all. It's time you started enjoying life and I just decided to help it along. I didn't know Pig was going to rear his head again but I wouldn't back his chances against Ross.' She gave Helen a hug. 'When's the wedding?'

'I said no,' Helen informed her steadily, and Tina's face was a mixture of disbelief and despair.

'You didn't! Oh, Helen, I give up on you, really I do. Men like Ross Maclean are rare and now he's got away. You would have been happy. We all would.' She stood and walked to the door, turning to look at Helen ruefully. 'I thought you could live again, live outside this little clan, but maybe I was wrong. The sister I knew seems to have gone for good.'

It hit Helen deeply and made her look at herself long and hard as she went to bed. The mirror only told her what she already knew. Inside she was frozen, holding tightly to the shaky security of being herself. Tina had said that the sister she knew had disappeared and Helen knew she was right. She lived behind a wall of fear and ice. Maybe she would never come out again? It had all seemed to be temporary at one time, a little while before she regained her self-esteem, her joy in living, but now it seemed to be her future image.

Her mind strayed unbidden to Ross, to the way she had felt when he kissed her, her cheeks growing hot. She had no idea now whether it was natural or not. Miles had left her in no doubt that she was very unnatural, frigid, ice-water cold. She hadn't felt like that with Ross in that lonely house. There was more to being married than kissing, though. She shuddered, her mind pushing away the vile attention that Miles had forced on her. Could she believe that Ross would leave her alone?

In the morning a letter dropped on to the mat, a long white envelope that made her fingers tremble as she opened it. Miles had started already. His solicitor explained the details, the new circumstances and told her that out of courtesy he was acquainting her with the facts. Miles intended to fight for Tansy. It was no cruel threat. It was cruel reality.

She rang Ross, her heart pounding painfully when he came on the line, so much so that for a second she couldn't speak.

'I—I've had a letter,' she told him when he had stiffly acknowledged her.

'It happens to the best of us,' he informed her sardonically. 'The mail arrives with boring regularity.'

In this mood she couldn't talk to him and she nearly put the phone down, but the night had been long and Tina's face had been drawn and set this morning. She had to continue.

'It was from a solicitor acting for Miles. He intends to go ahead.'

'I imagined he would, at this stage. After all, he hasn't had any fun out of the situation yet.'

'Help me, Ross!'

The words burst out like a despairing cry and there was silence for a minute before he said quietly, 'How can I? I'm merely your ex-boss, Helen.'

She closed her eyes, clenching her hands tightly, summoning up her courage. 'About what you said. If you meant it, if you still mean it, then I accept.'

'You'll marry me?'

'Yes. I can't run really, can I? It would all happen again, as you told me. He might win and I couldn't bear that. I'll marry you.'

'In that case,' he said softly, 'I'll be there in about half an hour.'

He put the phone down and Helen sat looking at it, her hands coming to her mouth in an unconscious gesture of anxiety. Had she done it again? Had she walked yet another time into a nightmare? If she had, then this time she had no excuse. Ross had laid it all on the line, right down to her sleeping arrangements.

'He's come back.' Tina turned to Helen in a belligerent mood as the car stopped at the gate. 'He's not given up. Don't turn him down, Helen. You'll regret it.'

She pounced out to answer the door before Helen could speak and she decided to keep quiet anyway. She had not told Tina about the solicitor's letter. There was now no need for her to know.

She got up and faced Ross with a certain amount of embarrassment when Tina let him in. He just stood and looked at her steadily, watching the colour flood under her skin, and Tina looked both anxious and awkward.

'Do you want me to go out? I can take Tansy out and...' She took hold of Tansy's hand but Ross smiled down at the tiny girl, who watched him with huge blue eyes.

'It's bitterly cold out there.' He picked up Tansy with such an air of ease that for a second Helen was in a whirl of uncertainty. He looked natural, like a father. It was astonishingly unsettling. 'In any case,' he added, looking at Tina, 'we need you here, I think. You can help us plan a wedding.'

'You're marrying Ross?' Tina looked at Helen and then scowled ferociously. 'You said... Do you know what a bad night I've had?'

'She changed her mind,' Ross said smoothly. He put Tansy down and then sat beside her. 'We need a quick wedding discussion because it's going to happen in two weeks, and then we'll go and see the house you'll all be living in.'

'Me?' Tansy asked, trying hard to follow this conversation.

'Especially you,' Ross informed her softly, glancing up at Helen. His eyes held hers and he suddenly smiled. 'A church wedding or a civil ceremony?' he asked quietly.

'I—I don't think I have a lot of choice,' Helen said, colour flooding back into her cheeks. 'I've been married.'

'Is that what it was?' His looks taunted. 'Let's see what we can put up in comparison.' He looked seductive, his eyes veiled, and a shiver ran right down Helen's spine. Of course he was doing this for Tina's benefit, and in a way she was grateful to him. Tina was completely taken in. All the same, his presence was beginning to affect her more each time she saw him, it was beginning to be more and more difficult to look away from those silvery eyes that seemed to touch her like a live wire.

'Gosh! The excitement!' Tina chortled, breaking the spell. 'Go for a civil ceremony, chief, it's going to be freezing in any church.'

'Well, chief?' Ross asked, his lips twitching in amusement, his eyes moving over Helen's pink cheeks.

'Yes. I—I don't know. I can't think. I'm sure they won't let me marry in church.'

'Oh, I don't know. I imagine I could twist a few arms. If that's what you really want?'

'No.' Helen suddenly remembered Miles. They had married in church. It had been a mockery after all, and this marriage was not for love or anything like it. To love and to cherish was not something she wanted to say under a great arched roof. Her face clouded and Ross frowned for a split second, but he had the situation in hand and was not about to let it deteriorate.

'You can decide later,' he said firmly. 'I think Tina and Tansy should go and look at their new home. We'll go between snowstorms,' he added, looking out of the window at a very threatening sky. 'I have to get workmen into there at once if we're to move right in after the wedding, otherwise I'll be stuck at the White Bear while my family are here.'

'Family!' Tina trilled, scooping Tansy up. 'Come on, pet, I'll get your things.'

As she went out Ross looked at Helen and then came to stand close, his eyes intent on her face.

'Relax, Helen,' he said softly. 'I have every intention of taking care of all of you. From this moment on you can stop worrying and stop being afraid. Nothing can touch you. I'll see to that.'

'I—I thought that before, when I married Miles,' she said hesitantly, stopping when she realised how it would sound. She expected anger but there was none there as she looked up at him.

'Oh, I know there are a few ghosts to fight,' he agreed. His hands came to her shoulders with great care, his fingers closing warmly around the slender bone-structure. 'I don't believe in ghosts, though, so I don't anticipate too much trouble. This marriage will benefit both of us but there's no reason why it should be so cold-blooded that you'll feel under threat.'

Something in his voice brought her head up swiftly, suspicion and anxiety in her face. 'You said... You promised that...'

'I'll never demand anything that you're not more than capable of giving, Helen. Get your coat,' he finished quietly.

He let her go and Helen was surprised how light-hearted she suddenly felt. She was under the wing of his power, they all were, and strangely enough she never doubted his word—she never had done, right from the first time she had seen him.

Events swept her forward at an alarming speed. There was no time to change her mind and, in any case, it would have taken more courage than she possessed to do so. Tina was ecstatic, the fear and worry lifted from her face, her faith in Ross without limit. There were happy discussions about where to place their own furniture and Helen saw at once that Tina recognised home in the old house where they would live. Tansy was delighted with the size of her place, her little feet taking her at great speed from room to room.

With a dominance that left them all breathless, Ross ordered workmen in the day after Helen had agreed to the marriage. Money spoke loudly, after all, and as the house had been empty for only a little while the work was mostly small adjustments and decorating. The interior designers complained endlessly but work went on all the same, especially after Helen learned to copy the hard stare that Ross turned on anyone who appeared to be slacking. The success of that did a lot for her confidence.

She did not go back to work. Tina had regained her nerve now that Ross was to take over their problems but, all the same, Helen felt the need to be close to Tansy and Ross agreed. As far as she could tell he simply plucked a good secretary from one of the other offices and a gloomy phone call from Jeanette assured her that a dragon in spectacles now sat in Helen's chair. The whole building, she was told, simply buzzed with the news of the wedding and Helen felt again the shiver of apprehension when she realised that Ross had lost no time in making it very official.

She knew exactly how official it was when he called one evening at the end of the week with news that alarmed her. She had seen little of him. They were both busy, and as she opened the door for him it seemed to her that she was marrying a hard, handsome stranger. She experienced the same odd shiver of apprehension that had scared her when she had first seen him. Ross was no ordinary man. His wealth alone would have lifted him right out of her sphere even if he had not been so different, so commanding.

He had made no attempt to be close. Their meetings had been as businesslike as the office. Now, as he stepped inside the warmth of the house, she felt like backing away. He was once again as he had been when she had first seen him, his grey eyes pinning her, that crystal gaze leaping out towards her as he stepped inside.

They looked at each other for a second, Helen's eyes darkening with the flare of panic that came every time she realised how committed she was to this enigmatic man.

Tina, on her way downstairs from settling Tansy, greeted Ross with her usual enthusiasm. 'Don't mind me. You can give each other a hug while I put the kettle on.'

'Now that's very understanding,' Ross murmured, his arms snaking out to capture Helen's waist before she could move. 'As a sister-in-law you'll be very acceptable.'

He pulled Helen closer, his eyes at once warning and sardonic, and there was little she could to escape the inevitability of it. In public she would have to play the part anyway, and if Tina knew the true state of affairs she would not be so gloriously happy as she was now.

She tried to submit fatalistically, expecting him to give her a brief kiss and draw back as Tina left, but even as their lips met she knew her mistake. She seemed to be ringed by flame, feelings surging through her like a bush fire, panic flickering among the flames as she felt herself going down in the heat of it.

She stiffened, fighting her way back, but the arms that held her were implacable and she went right down the blazing path, her lips parting with an awesome inevitability as Ross crushed her against him, his tongue probing her mouth. There was no way she could hold back, he took from her everything he could get with masterful ease, his lips moving against hers slowly, dominating her.

She felt her body beginning to melt, to curve into him, her mind starting to swim, dazzled and torn by a storm of feeling. She sighed against his mouth, forgetting where she was, wanting much more, hungrily searching for something she had never had and only dreamed of long ago. He almost seemed to hear her thoughts. Unexpectedly his hand lifted and stroked down her cheek, his lips easing to gentleness.

'Wow!' When he let her go, Helen heard the gasp of sound that told her Tina was still there, and Ross lifted his dark head to shoot a brilliant glance towards the foot of the stairs where Tina stood transfixed.

'So what happened to the kettle?' he enquired wryly, and Tina shot off to the kitchen.

'Pardon me.' Her face was wildly pink and Helen's face was little better as Ross turned her to the sitting-room, apparently unmoved by the event that had left her dazed.

'I have news and I'd better tell you before Tina rushes back.'

'I don't think she's likely to rush,' Helen managed shakily but he ignored the comment, his manner as brisk as if nothing had happened at all.

'The wedding has slightly grown in size.' He sat down and looked at her so evenly that she began to feel she had imagined that devastating kiss, the way he had held her. 'I had a call from New York this afternoon. My parents are determined to come. They'll be here the day before the wedding.'

'Oh.' Helen looked at him numbly. She hadn't given a thought to in-laws. By the time she had married Miles there had been no in-laws on either side. Now she was faced with the idea of meeting people she had never seen before, wealthy people who had a very grand lifestyle. Ross had said his mother entertained a lot and she knew all about his father. Tom Maclean's hardness was a legend.

'What did they say?' Frantically her eyes sought his, looking for reassurance, but he simply shrugged and looked back, a stranger again.

'I didn't ask for their opinion. I made an announcement and they reacted accordingly.'

'Angrily?' she wanted to know. There was something inside her that wanted to grasp him, to be reassured, but he offered no reassurance. She felt coldly on the outside of things, almost an onlooker.

'They know better than that.' His smile was grim but all the same she had the feeling that he was expecting trouble, that he was angry himself. Hadn't he said that they wanted him to marry an American heiress? This was what the wedding was all about from his point of view, after all. Her eyes clouded with doubt and he noted it.

'My father is going to fold at the knees as soon as he sees you. As for my mother, she knows me well enough. She hasn't succeeded in bringing me to heel in thirty-five years and it's all too late now. There isn't a thing to worry about.'

'Where are they going to stay?' She wanted to keep them at arm's length at all costs. She had agreed to this marriage very unwillingly, the whole thing seeming almost academic, but now it began to look real and she wanted to hold it back, to deny it.

'They have two choices: stay in London and drive up, or sample the White Bear. I think one look at the White Bear and Mother will head back to London at top speed.'

Helen hoped so. If they stayed in London it would cut down the meeting times. She sat in silence, running worries past her mind at some speed. There seemed to be a lot of them.

'Heard from Gilford?' His voice was cool authority and Helen looked up quickly.

'No. Why? Have you?'

'Why should I?' he enquired drily. 'He doesn't know about me. That's a little surprise for him.' There was a cold glitter about his eyes that told Helen the surprise was planned as a shock, and she pushed aside her other problems. She had forgotten Miles since Ross had arrived but the threat was still there. If it hadn't been, she would have been at work now, smart, efficient and irritated by Ross Maclean. Instead, she was going to marry him. Her hand went to her mouth, her teeth nibbling at her nails,

and when she looked up he was watching, reading quite
clearly her hesitation and her anxiety.

'You're in this now, Helen,' he reminded her coldly.
'For better or for worse.' There was a finality about it
that held her fast, just as his icy gaze held her fast, and
she was glad to turn to Tina as she walked in with tea,
her cheeks still flushed but a happy gleam in her eyes.

As it turned out, the Macleans arrived two days before
the wedding. It was the week before Christmas and they
announced their intention of coming straight up.

'The White Bear it is, then,' Ross murmured sardonically as he came to inform Helen. 'We're having lunch
with them today. It will give Mother the chance to get
over her hysteria and condemn the White Bear.'

Helen wondered what sort of woman this was who
had hysterics and yet held large parties. She had built
into her mind a very forbidding picture of them and as
she walked into the old inn with Ross she wondered if
he had been transmitting his own thoughts to her again.
They looked formidable and they were not alone.

'So this is the girl?' Tom Maclean's face gave nothing
away. Like Ross he was tall, handsome and autocratic-
looking, his thick hair white and well groomed. He
exuded the same aura of wealth, his eyes piercingly blue.
For a moment Helen thought he would make no move
to come forward. He had one hand in his pocket, his
easy stance telling its own story.

'This is Helen,' Ross assured him. They were almost
like two powerful animals, circling for advantage, each
obviously aware of the other's dangerous qualities, and
she was so enthralled by this attitude that she flinched
as Tom Maclean suddenly moved, coming forward to
take her hand.

'A blue-eyed beauty,' he said, his face relaxing a little. He glanced up keenly at Ross. 'I hope this child knows what she's letting herself in for. She realises, I hope, that you'll one day be head of a multi-million-dollar company? A cottage in the country is no possibility for you.'

'She knows all the drawbacks,' Ross replied sardonically. 'It's no use trying to put her off. We're engaged, it's official and we'll be married two days from now.'

'I'm not trying to put her off,' Tom Maclean murmured just as sardonically. 'I can safely leave that to Dee.'

It was clear that her future mother-in-law was not about to step forward. She looked utterly out of place in this old inn. The low beams were blackened and gleaming with age, a great fire roared against the cold outside, a Christmas tree glittered in the corner and the whole building had an old-world elegance, in spite of the predictability of the food.

Deirdre Maclean had a glitter of her own, diamonds and spite, Helen decided. She was beautiful, middle-aged, perfectly groomed and made up. In a slim-fitting suit of dark red, a mink coat draped carelessly around her shoulders, she looked outraged at her surroundings and equally outraged at her son's fiancée.

Suddenly Helen was very glad of the heavy diamond ring on her finger, a ring that until now she had felt out of place and rather frightening. Deirdre Maclean resented her and she needed all the security she could get.

A warm strong arm came round her shoulders and Ross urged her forward.

'We might as well get it over with,' he murmured drily. 'She's chosen her stance, right beside the Christmas tree and away from the nasty revealing lights.'

Helen shot a look at Tom Maclean as Ross uttered these derisive words but he was still standing there, his arrogant amusement apparent in the cold blue eyes.

'This is Deirdre,' Ross announced, his lips twisting ironically. 'Hold your hand out nicely, Helen. There's a chance she'll shake it.'

'I'm your *mother*, Ross!' Dee Maclean snapped, her eyes flashing with annoyance.

'You surprise me. I can't really believe that. Any mother of mine would be happy to meet my fiancée.'

'I am happy to meet her. Really, Ross, you're impossible.' She leaned forward and pecked at Helen's cheek, leaving behind a trail of exclusive perfume, and Ross gave a snort of laughter before turning to the other member of the party.

'What brings you to this cold little place, Donna?' he enquired with the same taunting edge to his voice.

His tone brought an angry blush to the cheeks of the girl who had stood steadfastly beside his mother.

'Maybe I came to take one last look at you.'

'Donna Street, Helen,' Ross introduced. 'An old friend of the family.'

'An old friend of Ross,' the girl corrected, her eyes still not leaving his darkly handsome face.

So this was the girl they had wanted him to marry? She was beautiful, blonde and exotic, clearly a product of the same wealthy background. The eyes that flickered over Helen's were almost black, filled with anger and distress. They lingered on Helen's ring and then moved with cold deliberation all over Helen's clothes.

'Does she know what being a Maclean means?'

'Ask her,' Ross suggested in amusement. 'She speaks English.'

'She looks scared, darling. I thought you were holding her upright.' The voice was filled with very sweet spite, and Ross tightened his arm around Helen's shoulders.

'I'm just holding on to her firmly. It occurred to me that after one look at this family gathering she might just walk out. In England we keep our displeasure tastefully hidden.'

'You're American! You don't belong here!' Donna snapped, her sweet amusement suddenly deserting her.

'And to think I never noticed,' he mocked. 'Have you ordered?' he added, glancing at his father.

'No. I thought we'd wait for you.'

'Then let's order now,' Ross suggested, signalling to a waiter who hovered in the background. 'There's a restaurant here. With any luck, there may be some left-over quiche,' he murmured to Helen.

She was too tightened up to be amused. It was not normal to be disliked so much but she could see the reason for it. Donna was a protégée of Deirdre Maclean, the girl she had chosen as suitable for Ross, and Donna was obviously in love with him, hurt and furious to meet his English fiancée. What Tom Maclean thought was impossible to decide. Like Ross he was cool, enigmatic and powerful. Any displeasure he felt would be worked off in action, not words. She realised that she had not said one single word as yet.

'Do you live in this—little village, Helen?' Deirdre Maclean asked politely as they sat down to eat. Her attitude suggested that she expected as much and looked upon it with despair.

'No. Two villages away, as a matter of fact.' Helen had made up her mind that she was not about to be browbeaten, and she saw a quick smile flit across Ross's lips as he heard her tone of voice.

'You were his secretary,' Deirdre pointed out almost accusingly.

'Well, that's why I'm marrying her,' Ross assured his mother. 'A good secretary knows all your secrets. Dad can vouch for that.'

Helen expected an angry retort but Tom Maclean's face was filled with wry amusement. Evidently he was used to these skirmishes. Helen wasn't and it was beginning to annoy her. She set her lips firmly and ate her meal.

'We should have brought our own family along, Helen,' Ross said with elaborate regret. 'We're out-numbered here.'

'You have a family, Helen? I was sure that Ross had said your parents were no longer alive.' Deirdre Maclean was instantly alert, ready to snoop, and Helen took a long, firm breath.

'I have a small family. My sister and my daughter.'

The announcement fell into a pool of silence. It seemed to ricochet from one to the other. Donna's eyes were fastened on Ross with sheer disbelief and Deirdre froze.

'You have a *child*!' Deirdre Maclean stared at Ross as if he were certifiable and he raised cool dark brows.

'Tansy is three. A quick calculation will tell you that she's not mine—yet. She's going to be, though. If I play my cards right she'll let me have her cast-off teddy-bear pyjamas.'

All at once Tom Maclean started to laugh. He had a loud laugh, unexpectedly pleasing, and his eyes were no longer cold as he looked at Helen.

'A ready-made granddaughter. Is she going to be at this wedding, then? I'd like to see her. I always wanted a daughter but Dee's figure was too important. What's your sister like?' He looked at Helen with a new-found interest. 'Is she a beauty, too?'

'She is,' Ross assured him. 'It runs in the family. Watch out for Tina, though, she doesn't have Helen's gentle ways. She'll eat you for breakfast and never notice it. Back off there.'

'I can hardly wait.' Tom Maclean chortled. 'I guess I'm looking forward to this wedding after all.'

'Returning to your roots?' Ross asked slyly.

'It's running through my mind.'

'You'll never leave America!' Deirdre said hotly, her outraged eyes moving from Helen to her husband.

'We'll see.' The way he said it reminded Helen of Ross, coldly taunting, sure of himself. 'I guess I'm going to have grandchildren, one adopted and plenty real, and I'll want to see them. I reckon Helen is a bit too English to settle in the States.'

'Then it's going to be an odd marriage,' Donna Street put in triumphantly, smiling across knowingly. 'Maybe she should think again? Maclean International is in New York. Ross will have to be there.'

'He won't,' Tom Maclean informed her shortly. 'I'm there. Ross is working to a plan. Europe's about to boom and we're pushing hard to get right in. Time's coming when I'll want to come home. I'm building up this end.'

'And what do I do?' Deirdre forgot all about Helen, an unhappy anger on her face.

'Why, honey, you'll adjust,' her husband told her with that sort of cool, indifferent assurance that informed Helen he would not step aside from any plans. She also knew that all was not well in this family. Ross was happier with her own little family, probably because they were so close-knit, and the thought warmed her as she would never have imagined. Was he lonely? Did he really need this marriage far more than he had admitted? She glanced across at him and he was watching her. Their eyes met and held and for a moment she thought she read something there of a deep unhappiness. It was fleeting, probably imagined, but it made him human, understandable, and for the first time ever she smiled into his eyes.

CHAPTER SEVEN

THE wedding was three days before Christmas Eve, a civil ceremony after all, and Helen's nerve held out only because Tina was so enthusiastic. Standing beside Ross, in a deep blue suit that deepened the blue of her eyes, a spray of orchids pinned across the lapels, she felt the need to run, to escape while she could, but although the thought of Miles and his threats kept her standing and answering, making her promises, she had the certain feeling that Ross knew.

He was more than usually silent, a silent domination that was almost menacing, and only when the ceremony was over and they were speeding to the reception in his car did he in any way relax.

'Hungry?' He glanced partly over his shoulder at Tina and Tansy on the back seat, and Tansy nodded vigorously. She had been quiet and rather overawed at the event itself, not understanding anything but feeling the tension as surely as a child picked up unusual vibes. Now she was unwilling to speak at all.

'She's only dumbstruck,' Tina observed as Helen glanced round a little anxiously. 'You've got to admit, chief, it was—an event.'

It had been an event. Deirdre Maclean had bristled with hostility, her duties as a witness performed grudgingly and very stiffly. Tom Maclean had seemed to delight in both the event and his wife's discomfiture, and Tina had witnessed it all from her seat at the back of the room with Tansy on her knee.

Donna Street had come too, her eyes disparaging and icy as Ross made his vows, her silence as telling as any announcement. She had barely responded to Tina's greeting and Tansy had openly cringed at her hostility.

'Your foot is well on the way to your mouth,' Helen warned quickly, not looking at Ross.

'Keep it moving in that direction,' Ross suggested wryly. 'Maybe we should have had a big wedding with plenty of guests to drown out the acid looks.'

'Who cares?' Tina asked blithely, her normal attitude to life restored under the protective canopy of Ross and his power. 'You're married. It's wonderful. Let them all come. We'll take them on!'

Ross began to laugh softly, flashing Tina a look of approval through the rear-view mirror. 'I like to hear fighting talk. Will you "take them on"?' he added softly, for Helen's ears alone.

'I don't think they're going to concern me,' she said quietly. 'I long ago learned to ignore what I don't like.'

She felt him stiffen by her side and wished back her thoughtless words. She needed Ross. They all did, but it was useless to pretend that this was an ordinary marriage and that her mother-in-law had upset her. She had been too filled with doubts and worried to really contemplate Deirdre Maclean's antagonism.

'Yes. Out of one safe nest into another,' Ross murmured coolly. 'Well, it's legal now, Helen. And final,' he added under his breath.

She heard him, though, and it occurred to her that he was not quite as happy about the arrangement as he had appeared to be. Perhaps seeing Donna again had unsettled him. It brought her out of her own attitude, a shiver of unease washing over her. How would she cope with this marriage? What sort of life had Ross planned for himself? She had thought only of her own problems, of safety for Tansy. Would he really be content to settle for that?

Having met his parents she had doubts about his words. Tom Maclean might be a determined and powerful man but he had indicated that his plans had been made with Ross. If anyone was pushing for their own way it was Deirdre, and she had no hold on Ross whatsoever as far as Helen could tell. She glanced at him anxiously but all she saw was a hard, handsome profile, cold grey eyes fixed on the road.

They were driving to a small reception in a restaurant quite a few miles from town, and the others had gone on ahead. What were they thinking? Were they as completely taken in by this as Tina? Today she moved into her new home. By tomorrow evening all her own things would be there, arranged as she and Tina had planned. The door on the past was closed, Miles shut out, but her safety brought with it worries she had long lost. She would have to share her life with Ross and it alarmed her.

The 'quiet' reception was a crowded affair, the private room full to overflowing as they walked in, and Donna drifted forward to smile up at Ross with a look of triumph.

'Surprise, darling!' she greeted. 'It seemed such a lonely little meal to have planned, just the seven of us. I got in touch with a few of our friends after lunch the other day. I knew you'd want to introduce Helen and your ready-made family.'

'You're so thoughtful.' Ross glanced round the room. It seemed to Helen that there were at least forty people there and she felt Tansy clutch at her skirt. There was no need to have Donna's action explained. She was showing Ross how foolish he was, how he was tying himself down. He turned to Tansy but Helen got there first, picking her up and holding her close.

'Go and meet your friends,' she advised Ross with a cool smile. 'I'll give Tansy all the moral support she needs.'

'I know who my friends are.' His lips were tight and annoyed, his eyes telling her that he had not missed the way she had cut him out. He reached out and deliberately took Tansy into his arms, turning to Tina. 'Come along, sister-in-law. We'll come back for the bride in a minute.'

It gave Donna the chance she was looking for. 'Did I do the wrong thing?' she asked archly as Ross pushed his way into the laughing crowd. 'I thought he would like to see his buddies. Quite a few of us are in London.'

'Really? I thought you flew in with his parents?'

'Oh, this time I did, but I'll stay, of course. I'm never far away from Ross. We're too—entwined to be separated for long.'

'Of course,' Helen said coolly. 'An old family friend. I know just what you mean. It must be a comfort for him. I can see how much he's enjoying it.'

She couldn't help a little smile. Ross looked on the edge of murder, his face darkening when he looked up and saw her in close conversation with Donna. He came back quickly, handing Tansy over and pulling Helen to the laden tables.

'I don't know about the bride,' he growled, 'but the bridegroom's hungry.'

'You always were insatiable, Ross.'

Donna's comment brought a wry smile to his face.

'But then, we know each other so well, don't we?' He took Helen's arm again and led her off, but she was not deceived at all even if she had been meant to be. There was more than friendship here. Donna Street had intended to marry Ross and she was not about to give up now. The small matter of his marriage to Helen was apparently dismissed as a minor hitch.

Helen was glad to see the end of the reception. She had spoken to people she would never meet again, had smiled until her face was stiff, and Tansy was fretful, intimidated by the crowd. She couldn't seem to find Tina and was relieved finally to see her talking to Tom Maclean. She signalled discreetly. Ross had gone to fetch the car round to the front. It was time to go and she slipped into the comparative quiet of the foyer to wait, Tansy snuggled to her shoulder.

'Why have you done this, Ross? You knew I'd come over to you as soon as you got settled in England. It wasn't all that much of a quarrel.'

Helen stopped dead as she heard Donna's voice, a softly pleading tone in it that she had not heard before. They were standing by a small alcove set into the foyer and the gloom of a snowy afternoon made Helen almost invisible to them, completely invisible as they were intent solely on each other.

'Our lives have been made up of a series of quarrels,' Ross pointed out sardonically. 'The last was just another along the way. It didn't influence me.'

'It influenced you enough to rush into this marriage.' Donna's words trembled, close to tears. 'Just because you've been sleeping with her——'

'Helen is as pure as driven snow,' Ross interrupted in obvious amusement.

'You mean she's frigid? She looks it with that icily composed face, that impossible "old maid" hairdo. She's so different from us, darling.'

'She's got everything I want.' His voice was darkly quiet, still amused, and Helen heard Donna catch her breath.

'A family! You devil! You're just like Tom. A family is a good shield, isn't it?'

'You've got a wild imagination, Donna.'

'Wild enough to know you'll want me around, and I'll be here, Ross. I'm not going away.' She flung her arms around his neck, pressing a long kiss against his lips, and Ross was laughing softly as he held her away.

'I never imagined you would, honey. I know your every move. Do you think I didn't expect you?'

Helen stepped slowly back into the crowded room. Tansy was sleeping against her and Helen clutched her tightly, clinging to what she had. Inside a pain had flowered, a pain she had never felt before in her life, jealousy twisting and turning. She had felt sick as Ross held Donna, physically ill. She looked round blindly for Tina, wanting to get away without Ross, knowing it was impossible. She had stepped from behind her wall of safety only to rediscover that it was frightening and painful outside.

The house had been done beautifully. Ross had given Helen a free hand with the furnishing and she had not been foolish enough to go against the advice of the well-known firm of interior designers he had engaged. The treasured antiques that belonged to Tina and herself had impressed them and gradually, as the days had raced along, the small cottage that had been home for so long had emptied as their own furniture had been placed carefully among the new furnishings of the house. Everything blended perfectly, the hard work that Helen had put in very worth while, and as they came back to the house they would call home Tina's face was worth all the effort.

'It's home,' she murmured to Helen, tears in her eyes. 'Dad would have liked this.'

They were giving each other a consoling hug when Ross came back into the hall, a plump, motherly woman in tow.

'Mrs Hill, our housekeeper, Helen,' he introduced quietly. 'Mrs Hill, my wife, Helen, and my sister-in-law, Tina.'

Helen had thought that surprises were over but here he was again, astonishing her. She barely had time to come to her senses and shake the outstretched hand before Mrs Hill was crouching in front of Tansy, her pleasant face creased in smiles.

'My, you're a little picture,' she said warmly.

'Tansy, our daughter,' Ross informed her firmly, his narrowed eyes amused as Helen looked up in amazement.

'She's the picture of you, Mrs Maclean. Not at all like her father.'

'Not in any way at all,' Helen agreed wryly.

'Amen!' Tina muttered and, although Mrs Hill looked a bit startled, Ross was looking very pleased, the smile in his eyes growing.

'Can I go to my new room?' Tansy wanted to know as Mrs Hill went off to the kitchen to make tea, and Tina stepped forward with her usual enthusiasm.

'Me too. I'm right next door, pet. All your toys are here. I want to sort out my clothes.'

As they went up the curved stairs, Helen looked at Ross, finding his eyes on her face, his mouth twisted ironically.

'What do I do with a housekeeper?' she asked with only mild exasperation. 'I've never managed one in my life.'

'You'll cope,' he assured her. 'I've seen you come the heavy with plenty of people in the office, including me. Mrs Hill looks thoroughly docile. In any case, you're not here to become a domestic drudge. This house is just

too big. Tansy needs you, Tina needs you and so do I.
We can't have you spread too thin on the ground, can
we? You're the hostess, not the kitchen maid. And you're
my wife.'

The determination with which he said that had a shiver
running over Helen, and it did nothing to relax her when
she muttered that she would change and he moved beside
her up the stairs, obviously going in the same direction.
She hadn't been in the house for quite a few days. Getting
things out of the cottage and out of the store had
occupied a lot of her time just before the wedding, and
Ross had volunteered to order the finishing touches. She
was a bit lost.

'I don't know quite where I am,' she admitted, a little
flustered. She had deliberately arranged rooms for Tina
and Tansy and had put off her own arrangements. She
had been too uneasy to discuss it with Ross. Now she
was more embarrassed than ever.

'We're here.' Ross opened a door and motioned her
inside.

'We?' She stopped on the threshold, shying away like
a startled colt, but his hand behind her back urged her
on, giving her no option but to go into the huge room
that faced the gardens at the front.

'Save the panic,' he ordered drily. 'This is your own
room. Mine is here.' He threw open communicating
doors and Helen looked through into the other room
that faced the front.

'You said I would have my own room,' she began, but
he came to stand in front of her, looking at her as if she
were a child and barely in control of her tongue.

'You have your own room, Helen. This is it. I'm next
door. Did you want me to be at the other end of the
house or would you have liked me to choose a nice
broom-cupboard? Today we were married. Mrs Hill

called you by your married name not two minutes ago. I'm prepared to go along with your fears and worries, with your terror of men, but only so far. I'm not prepared to either look like an idiot or upset Tina.'

'Tina?' Helen looked up at him and he looked coldly back.

'Surely you remember her? Your sister. The bright young girl who is so sure that we're madly in love with each other. Just think how disappointed she would be to find you here in splendid isolation. If she saw me disentangling myself from the mops and brushes each morning she'd burst into tears.'

'Very funny!' Helen snapped. 'Tina won't know a thing. She'll not come in here.'

'Wrong, wrong, wrong,' he sighed, apparently filled with exasperated weariness. 'Your little family circle is too tightly knit to have zones that are off-limits. The only way she'll stay out of here is if she thinks it's my room too. Hence my determination to be next door. Our arrangement is supposed to be a secret and that means Tina doesn't know either.'

'Of course she won't know!' Helen glared at him, working up anger to hide her misgivings, her pounding heart. 'However, I know my sister. How long do you think it will be before she discovers another room—with you in it?'

'She'll imagine it's how the very rich live,' he said blandly. 'In any case, she may not discover it at all. Perhaps we'll change our arrangement before then and we'll both be next door.'

'You promised!'

Helen looked up quickly, her blue eyes wide and purple-shadowed and he smiled like a satisfied tiger, linking his arms around her waist so that she had to lean back on them to get anywhere away from him.

'Ah! The return of the terror. I said I would never ask you to do anything you were not capable of.'

'I'll never be capable of——'

The sentence was unfinished, her sharp words stopped as his lips covered her own and he drew her fully into his arms. She fought furiously even though her heart threatened to pound right out of her body. It wasn't disgust. It was jealousy. How long ago had it been since Donna Street had been pressed close to him, kissing him? He tightened her to him, trapping her arms, his hand closing possessively behind her head, his lips never leaving hers, and all the fight went out of her.

He was too strong to fight, too powerful. She almost sagged against him, feeling the hungry need again that rose so sharply with no warning, and his hands lost their cruel grip as he stroked her closer to him, his whole body seeming to enclose her.

She was still not fighting as he planted tiny kisses along her neck and jaw and, when his lips returned to hers, her own mouth parted to accommodate him.

'What are you not capable of, Helen?' he asked softly and triumphantly, his eyes dazzling her as he raised his head. 'All you have to do is let the ice melt.'

She seemed to be incapable of doing anything but look back into his eyes, a gasp of shock leaving her parted lips as his hand came warmly and possessively to her breast. He was holding her so closely, so securely, that she never flinched, her reaction one of almost pained wonder. His eyes held hers as he stroked over the tilted perfection through the thin white silk of her blouse, and she moaned under her breath as his fingers found the throbbing centre, manipulating it into singing life.

Shudders seemed to be racing over her, sweet, painful and exciting, and her eyes closed in self-defence because there was no other way she could escape him—her body refused to move.

'Why are you doing this?' she whispered shakily.

'Only to straighten you out.' His voice was mocking, close to her ear, and he gave the smooth lobe a tiny nip with white, even teeth. 'I can't have you fainting every time I need to hold you, can I? People will get suspicious.' His hand left her breast, moving to enclose her throat, his thumb tilting her chin. He studied her face and smiled a long, slow smile. 'Are you going to accuse me of forcing you? Or can't you move?'

Colour flooded into her pale face and he released her, putting her from him with a sort of quiet deliberation that told her the experiment was finished.

'I've got something for you,' he said evenly, no sign of the agitation about him that Helen felt. He nodded towards the bed where she was to sleep, the covers drawn back to reveal silk sheets. There was a long velvet box and, when she simply stood where he had left her, he picked it up and opened it, taking out an expensive gold watch and fastening it on her limp wrist.

'A wedding present,' he murmured quietly, 'or did you think the present was Mrs Hill?'

'Thank you. It's beautiful.' Helen had never had a gold watch before and she looked down at it with a sort of childlike wonder. He moved to the door and she looked up then, wanting him to stay, admitting it to herself with fright.

'Ross. I—I have something for you.'

The dark brows rose in surprise and he stopped in the doorway.

'For me? What?'

'A—a present. I—I didn't know what to get because you've got so much and...'

'So you decided to give me Tansy,' he mocked. The mockery was soft though and she took heart, going to the bed and searching in her bag, coming out with a small box.

'I should have given you this before, or—or even today when... It may not fit.'

He looked at her for a minute, his eyes intently searching her face, and then he took the small box and opened it, looking down at the plain golden ring inside, saying nothing. She almost panicked then. To give him a wedding-ring was too much. *Now* she knew it. It had been more than an impulse, though. After meeting his parents at the White Bear, seeing their almost open animosity to each other and the brittle way that Deirdre treated Ross, she had been angered for him. Her own parents had loved openly, showered unselfish affection on both Tina and herself. She had seen his face, seen the flash of loneliness, and the ring had been a gesture, an almost possessive gesture welcoming him into her own small family. She should never have done it. She could see that now.

'A wedding-ring. It can't be anything else, can it?'

Ross looked up at her as he said the words, catching the expression in her eyes, eyes that were enormous and anxious.

'Put it on,' he ordered softly, placing the ring in her palm and holding out his hand.

'I—I suppose I shouldn't have... After all, this isn't real.'

'Put it on, Helen.'

She slid the ring on to his finger, surprised that it seemed to be a perfect fit. He flexed his hand experimentally and looked down at the ring, before taking her hand and gazing for a minute at the rings he had given her.

'For better or for worse,' he murmured quietly. He raised his eyes, watching her for a minute, and then he smiled, a slow, beautiful smile. 'Why?' he asked softly.

'I told you. I couldn't think what to get and...'

Ross laughed quietly, a low sound in his throat. 'Helen, Helen,' he admonished in an amused voice, 'when the ice melts you'll be quite a woman. Until then, I can wait.'

'There's nothing to wait for,' she managed hastily, colour flooding her face. In fact she was pleased, pleased with his reaction to her gift, pleased with the unusual soft amusement in his voice.

'But there is,' he assured her, his strong hand tilting her face. 'When you're perfectly normal, free of panic, all the ice melted, then let me know, because I want you. That's what I'm waiting for.'

He was gone before she could react, and she was glad because her reaction was utterly predictable. To be kissed, held, caressed by Ross was one thing, an excitement she had never known before, but for him to want her, to expect a real wife, was another thing entirely. She knew that one kind of rapture could never lead to another with her. Miles had proved that to her without any doubt at all. It was something she could never face again, never even think about. If Ross expected that then he was doomed to be waiting forever. She was a cripple as far as that was concerned.

The room next door would never know two people, not if one of them had to be her. The fact that sprang into her mind then had her hands clenching tightly, her nails biting into the palms. Donna Street was perfectly normal, she too was used to his arms, his kisses, and much more. That was why she was here, in England: to see that a normal man got normal affection.

Helen's face set in the old, old lines of cool control and she went downstairs for the tea that Mrs Hill had served. Ross glanced at her, but apart from the fact that his dark brows rose sceptically he might not have ever been close to her. He was very adept at reading her mind and he had recognised her closed expression. It was as well, Helen thought bitterly. He would know not to wait for anything.

After the tea he went to his newly set-up study and came back with two long envelopes, tossing Helen and Tina one each.

'I've opened accounts for you at the same bank,' he told them. 'Here are the forms to sign and all the details. Tomorrow you'll have to go in, give your signatures and see the branch manager. Your credit cards should be there to pick up.'

'Ross!' Tina gave a shriek of astonishment and Helen just looked at him, unable to say anything at all.

'You,' Ross said, looking firmly at Tina, 'have a credit limit. I don't want to see you dressed in cloth of gold.'

As usual they were grinning at each other and Helen was once again struck by how close they seemed to be. Her eyes fell to the ring she had given him and she knew most surely that he was part of them—more than that, she knew he was part of herself.

'Mrs Maclean, of course,' he was continuing, 'can spend without limit. I have faith in her common sense.'

'I'm insulted,' Tina said blithely.

'You're only the sister-in-law, child. Count your blessings.'

'I do, Ross,' she suddenly said solemnly. 'I've not been so happy for years, not since... Oh, damn!' Tina suddenly stood and almost raced out of the room, her eyes filled with tears, and Helen knew just exactly why. Nothing would ever be allowed to hurt Tina again.

'I've upset her?' Ross looked at her and Helen shook her head.

'Memories. Some bad, some good. This house...' She shrugged, fighting off her own ghosts and winning. 'You're very good to her.'

'I married her sister,' he pointed out a little tightly, 'and while we're on the subject,' he continued, a hardness entering his tone, 'you can leave Tansy with Tina and Mrs Hill one day and go for a shopping trip to London. Buy as many clothes as you need and order more.'

'But why? I've got a wardrobe filled with clothes. I haven't even got them all here yet.'

'Anything that Gilford bought you can be thrown out,' he said bitingly. 'Get enough to manage with over Christmas and deal with the rest immediately afterwards. I want nothing in this house that he paid for, whatever his murky reasons.' He stood up and glared down at her. 'And if you think I'm being a domineering brute, then that's about right!'

He walked out leaving her almost open-mouthed, and she didn't know whether to be delighted or furious. In the end she decided to be understanding. After all, with every garment she wore that Miles had paid for she had a wave of shuddering memories, all like nightmares. A man as proud and imperious as Ross would not like to think that she was wearing things that had been used to bedazzle clients.

She would do everything he asked. Maybe she could get a day to herself and still plan a good Christmas? With a housekeeper here she would have time to decorate a tree, to shop and do plenty of things, even though it was now dangerously close to Christmas Eve. She suddenly felt happy, until she began to wonder if Ross would invite his parents for Christmas, along with Donna. There was the chance that his mother and father would have returned to New York but there was no chance of Donna leaving. With her own ears she had heard a declaration to the contrary. Donna Street would stay where Ross was, giving him the comfort a man needed, a comfort she had obviously given him before, his new family a very good cover, just like his father. She had heard those words too and suddenly she began to see Deirdre's brittle anger in a new light, because she felt the growing of a similar anger herself.

CHAPTER EIGHT

IT WAS obvious that Ross meant exactly what he had said because the next day Helen found he had arranged to take her to London. Tina had elected to stay and care for Tansy with the valuable assistance of Mrs Hill, and there didn't seem to be one excuse to hand.

There was a sort of grim determination about Ross that made her fear he would personally supervise her shopping, but once in the city she was left to herself, a day of freedom before her and an unlimited amount of money at her disposal. Ross had business meetings to attend and could make no promise about lunch so she set off alone on a cold, crisp day.

The unusual freedom took some getting used to but after a while she began to enjoy herself. The words she had heard from Donna Street still seemed to be ringing in her mind, the 'old maid' hairdo comment still rankling, and she made that her first stop. She was lucky to get an appointment, but her nerve nearly deserted her as she saw the long black hair being attacked with ruthless skill. Even so, it gave a lift to her spirits, as if the weight of her hair had been holding her to the ground.

The final effect was worth the effort. The cleverly cut pageboy was just clear of her shoulders, shining, swinging and glossy. It fell in dark wings against her cheeks, blue-sheened and dramatic. It seemed to have altered her disposition because she went out into crowds with a smile on her face, her whole being light-hearted.

Ross had insisted that she left most of the clothes to be delivered and she saw the good sense of this as her purchases mounted steadily. She was meeting him for the journey back home but until then she was without help as far as carrying parcels was concerned. She had a coffee and caught a taxi to Russell Square, knowing she would be a little early but too excited about meeting him to worry about that.

Her mind never seemed to leave him at the moment. In spite of her fears she secretly longed to be back in his arms. He could arouse her so easily and it was something she had never felt before. Miles had taken no trouble to arouse her, no trouble to please her, his desire brutal, animal and cruel. There was nothing brutal about the hard arms that had recently held her; there was only excitement, a tempting danger, a rising hunger that left her empty afterwards.

She took out her small mirror, trying to see herself clearly, her heart beginning to flutter at the sight of her own flushed cheeks. She was behaving like a bride! It was madness. Nothing could come of it, after all. At this rate, Ross would see her weakness as soon as they met. She stopped the taxi.

'Here will do.'

'We're not there yet, miss.' The driver glanced over his shoulder but she smiled quickly and nodded.

'I know. I decided to walk the rest of the way. I'm too early.'

'As you like, love.' He pulled into the side of the road and Helen got out into the cold of the afternoon. This chill would take a bit of the steam from her, she thought with a wry smile as she set off on the short walk to her meeting-place.

She saw Ross almost at once. He was a man to draw the eye, his height and good looks making him stand out clearly from the crowds. And he wasn't alone. Donna Street was clinging to his arm, laughing up into his face, her smile self-satisfied as he hailed a taxi.

Helen stopped, panic-stricken that they should see her, a nearby doorway the only refuge. She wanted to run, to turn back and go the way she had come, but a perverse feeling of shame had her watching still as the taxi stopped and Ross handed his companion into it. Donna smiled up at him and then impulsively reached out, her arms encircling his neck, her lips pressed close to his. Helen looked away then, shaking and defeated.

What had she expected? He had told her he would have no shame in seeking female company and this particular female had announced her intention of staying well within reach. He could afford to wait, as he had said, because nothing was being denied him in the meantime.

'Helen?'

She had hurried around the corner, arriving before him, standing looking into a shop as he came up.

'I thought I was seeing things. You had that long hair cut.'

'I don't need to look so efficient now.' She couldn't smile. She hardly dared raise her eyes. It was stupid to feel so betrayed when she had insisted on having her own room, on having a very impersonal marriage, but she felt betrayed all the same. The whole reason for the marriage seemed to have changed so swiftly. Ross could hurt her and he didn't even know it.

'Do you feel all right?' His brilliant gaze moved over her face, caught the swinging shine of her hair as the winter sunlight flashed blue lights across it.

'Just tired. I've been on my feet for most of the day.'

'Then let's go home. I could do with a rest myself.'

He knew there was something specially wrong but he was not about to ask again. His crystal eyes had hardened, his firm mouth set uncompromisingly.

'Have you been in meetings all day?' She had to pry. Suddenly she wanted to scream at him, to accuse him, to sob out her jealousy, but she knew perfectly well she wouldn't.

'Most of the day.' His laconic reply didn't surprise her. What had she expected? He was hardly likely to tell her he had spent the day with Donna, perhaps in some hotel.

He was particularly silent, moodily so, and she was glad. It gave her the chance to collect her pride around her. She felt wounded, lonely, back where she had started but for a very different reason. On the way back it began to snow heavily, the wind rising to drive it along.

'A white Christmas. Tansy will get her snowman after all.'

'Yes. Tomorrow I'll decorate the tree.' Helen said nothing more, continuing to gaze out at the driving snow. It seemed that every wish uttered was to be granted. She had mentioned to Tina that the huge drawing-room would accommodate a high Christmas tree and next day it had been delivered. A sledge had come too, something she had vaguely murmured to Tansy when Ross had first come home with her for dinner. It was to be a golden cage, the bars of her own making because she was securely trapped by the past.

Christmas Day dawned clear and bright with a good covering of snow, at least two inches. The trees in the garden were a wonderland and Tansy's excitement seemed to get into them all. There were presents to unwrap, shrieks of delight from Tina as she opened the gifts around the tree, and Ross was warmly amused, crouching by Tansy to help with her own unwrapping.

'Let's try out the sledge,' Tina suggested eagerly as Mrs Hill came in to help clear away the brightly coloured wrappings. 'There's a super run in the next field.'

'Not me.' Ross stood and stretched like a great cat, unexpectedly reaching for Helen and helping her to her feet. 'If I'm to enjoy the rest of the day I have about an hour's paperwork to complete.'

'Don't you ever stop working?' Tina looked at him with mild exasperation. 'I had it in mind for you to push uphill.'

'Ah! Just as I suspected.' He grinned down at her. 'Paperwork is quieter, warmer and takes less energy.'

'Spoilsport! It won't be the same, will it, Helen?'

'I expect we'll manage.' She could feel his eyes on her, ironical and wryly questioning, and she wasn't going to draw him any closer. As she had watched him this morning she had felt the great heaviness on her heart, the unexpected surging again of misery. The other day there had been Donna. Helen couldn't pretend it hadn't happened.

She looked up and he was watching her as Tina made for the door with Tansy in tow, and he wasn't looking ironical at all. There was a sober look of understanding on his face.

'Keep behind your wall, Helen. It's safe enough there.' He glanced at the window, the bright glare of sun on snow making the room extraordinarily light. 'I'm not at all sure that it's cold enough for you out there,' he added flatly.

He walked out and Helen looked at the bracelet on her wrist, an expensive present from her husband. A cage of gold with bars of molten misery. She wouldn't let it happen! She didn't need more than his protection after all. She ran upstairs and changed into warm clothes, adding thick boots and an anorak, a red woollen cap pulled over her ears, and when Tina dragged the new sledge from the garage Helen was right there with her, pulling a wildly excited Tansy across the huge garden and into the adjoining field. *They* were her family, not Ross.

'It's hot work,' Tina complained as they dragged the sledge uphill for the tenth time. Tansy enjoyed the ride back as much as she enjoyed the wild trip downhill and Helen trudged uphill, Tansy on her back.

'Have a go, chief,' Tina suggested as they reached the top of the steep hill. 'We'll sit this one out.'

'Me?'

'You!' Tina looked at her sideways. 'Who knows, with a bit of luck it might bring out some Christmas spirit. You certainly know how to put a damper on things.'

Helen felt a swift surge of annoyance. She was doing her best! If they hadn't been here they would have all had a happy, relaxed Christmas. If things had stayed as they were she wouldn't have been trudging up the hill trying to smile and thinking about Donna Street. Fairness surfaced belatedly. They would probably have been hiding behind locked doors and dreading the arrival of Miles.

'You're on!' She looked with defiant haughtiness at Tina and manoeuvred the sledge into place. So far she had walked down the hill behind them as Tina had gone rapidly down with Tansy clutched close. What was the matter with her? She was twenty-four, not eighty-four. She flung herself face forward on to the sledge and pushed off.

It was steeper than she thought and the sledge went faster than she had expected. There was the sound of the runners on the crisp snow, the feel of wind in her ears and she heard the other two shrieking with delight. She ended up in deep snow by the hedge, rolling off and standing to give a self-satisfied little bow.

'Again, Mummy!' Tansy was delighted and Helen was startled to see the pleasure it had given her little daughter. Was she getting staid, bitter? Was it beginning to affect the way she dealt with Tansy even?

She didn't stop to think. She got back on and went down again but this time her mind was almost left behind, seeing herself with fresh eyes. She missed the snowbank by the hedge and went right through the gap, the sledge turning over, landing on top of her as all the breath left her body.

She seemed unable to move for a minute and that was all the time it took for Ross to lift the sledge free and look down at her vibrantly.

'Where do you hurt?' His voice sounded harsh, reprimanding, and she sat up, brushing snow from her jacket.

'I don't hurt at all.' She could see Tina plunging down the hill, Tansy in her arms. 'You must have eyes in the back of your head, and seven-league boots.'

He was dressed for the snow and yet she had left him indoors, working.

'I was almost here, as a matter of fact. I saw your first Cresta run—and your second.'

Now he wasn't making any attempt to help her and Helen stood up all by herself, instantly sliding back into the wet snow.

'Oh!'

'Now we know where you hurt.' His eyes glinted down at her. 'We'll begin again, I think.'

'I've twisted my ankle.' She looked up at him a bit desperately and he gave her a rather grim smile. Her red woollen cap was lying in the snow, her hair curved around her cheeks, blackbird wings of darkness against her flushed face. The vulnerability that her ankle made her feel was written in her eyes, and her crazy resentment, as if it were Ross who had arranged her fall.

'Are you all right?' Tina arrived breathlessly and Helen caught hold of her flying feelings, her acute sense of anger that Ross didn't belong to her.

'I'm perfectly all right. I twisted my ankle. Now I'll hobble indoors to the fire.'

'Pull Tansy in on the sledge,' Ross ordered. 'I'll deal with our injured athlete.'

That certainly dispelled Tina's worries and she went off grinning as Ross lifted Helen effortlessly and turned to the house.

'Do you have to control everything?' she spat at him, knowing she was being unfair but unable to cope for much longer. 'We've been managing our own affairs long before you came on the scene.'

'Storm away, Helen.' His face was grim and he didn't look at her, simply continuing towards the house. 'We've come a long way since you were the efficient Miss Andrews. A very peculiar shift in our relationship.'

'Not really. We're married for mutual defence but deep inside there's no change at all.'

'Perhaps you're right.' He sounded bored, weary of the conversation, and she felt like a spoiled child. He had done everything for them, surrounded them with his powerful protection, but she didn't feel protected. She felt restlessly uneasy, perilously close to tears.

'I can walk quite well. I didn't break a bone.'

'You should know. It's your ankle.' He lowered her to the snow-covered ground and pain twisted her lips at once. She turned her head but it was too late.

'I trust you've finished playing games?' He scooped her up and continued towards the house, ignoring the flush of embarrassment that flooded over her cheeks. She didn't know what to say to him any more. The thought of Donna Street was eating into her like acid. She wanted his arms to tighten around her but they didn't. He held her impersonally, merely as a kindness. She was perverse, mad, and she knew it. If he tightened his arms, looked at her as if he wanted her, she would be afraid.

Indoors he slid her to the floor, keeping her upright as she slipped off her anorak.

'You'll have to change—you're wet through. I'll get you upstairs.'

The cold observation brought a further burst of misery. Upstairs, to her *own* room. What was the matter with her? It was exactly what she had wanted, protection and no strings attached. She made no demur when he carried her upstairs.

'Do you need any help?' He set her down on a soft chair, looking at her with coolly indifferent eyes.

'No, thank you. If I need help I'll call Tina.'

'You won't.' His voice took on a sharpness that stung her. 'Tina expects your husband to help you to undress. That being the case, you manage or *I* help.'

'I can manage. I said that originally, I believe.'

Ross just turned and walked out of the room and she was suddenly bereft. This was a no-win situation, everything closing around her. She had never felt this for Miles even when she had first known him. He had pretended kindness, laughed, been considerate and gentle, all tricks to lull her senses.

Ross was imperious, in control of himself and everything around him. There was no pretence with Ross; the pretence was all on her side. She felt treacherous, her body dominating her mind. They had agreed on the sort of marriage this would be and now she was blaming him

for being exactly what she had wanted, his constant
generosity counting for nothing. She remembered how
she had felt protective towards him when she had
glimpsed sadness for one brief second. Shame flooded
over her, bringing tears to her eyes.

She pulled off her boots and struggled out of her thick
trousers, dropping them to the carpet, her sweater following as she dragged it over her head. It seemed a long
way to the wardrobe, even further to the bathroom, but
she managed to get a slip from a drawer and slide it over
her head.

She splashed her face with water and looked down at
her ankle. It was puffy, red. Probably it would be bruised
and purple tomorrow. It showed what happened when
she tried to be normal, to behave like a child instead of
a woman with responsibilities.

Tears streamed down her cheeks without her even
knowing. She didn't want responsibilities, not the
endless, unbroken responsibilities she had faced for so
long. She was tired, wound up, no longer capable of
giving off the icy cold image of efficiency. In the office
now she would have simply folded and gone under. Even
here there was no place to hide, not from herself.

It was ridiculous. A grown woman standing looking
at the dresses in her wardrobe and crying like an idiot,
hot silent tears that streamed down her face. She was
too upset to even decide what to put on.

'This.' A strong brown hand reached out and selected
a long dress of amethyst, one of her new dresses. 'It will
hide your ankle, keep you warm and please Mrs Hill,
who is fussing over a very elaborate Christmas lunch.'

Helen spun round, going off balance, too startled to
speak as Ross caught her and stood looking down at her
unhappy face.

'What are you...?'

'Doing in your room?' he finished for her. 'I don't know.' He shrugged and looked into her eyes. 'Maybe I'm doomed to help the weak and the lame. Right now, you're both.'

'I'm not dressed.' She began to wipe the tears away, her hand shaking, and he smiled wryly.

'I have normal vision. I'll just go on looking at your face.'

'I'm covered up.' She tried to sound loftily sure of herself but it came out something like a plea. His touch was light but it sent signals right through her, excitement beginning to rise over her misery.

'Reasonably so,' he agreed, glancing down at her slender figure in the lacy slip. 'There, you've spoiled it now. Until this moment I'd never noticed you.'

Even though he sounded wryly amused, there was a vibrant quality to his voice that had her looking at him with anxious eyes, her expression changing when she realised that her anxiety was that he would go. His gaze intensified, his eyes holding hers.

'How is the ankle?' He went on looking down at her and she couldn't speak for a second.

'It—it hurts like mad.'

'Then don't stand on it.'

He swung her into his arms, her figure slight against him, the silk of her skin as soft as the slip that covered her. Slowly his head bent and she made no move to turn her face away because she needed his kisses, his arms, his strength and the warm masculine feel of his body against hers.

Languorously her head fell back to the curve of his arm. She seemed so fragile against him, his strength too much for her, and his arms tightened.

'I'm going to kiss you, Helen.'

The dark voice was almost as exciting as his announcement and her eyes closed slowly, a breathless waiting about her that brought a low deep murmur to his throat. His mouth caught hers quickly, urgently, moving convulsively over hers, and she surrendered at once, her arms winding around his neck, slender and clinging. Without knowing it she arched her body, pressing closer.

He crushed her against him then, moving to the chair, settling her on his knee, the kiss unbroken. It was like a whirlwind, a crackling fire, a soaring sensation of light and heat that lifted her away from the room. All she could do was feel, thoughts and anxieties forgotten. His lips parted and Ross accepted her sweetness, draining everything from her, leaving her shaken and aching.

His breathing was heavy as he at last lifted his head, his lips slowly releasing hers. The eyes that looked down at her transformed face were a blaze of silver, lights flickering across them.

'Now are you ready for me?'

He watched her flushed face, the frantic pulse beating at the base of her white throat, and her eyes slowly opened, dazed, purple and luminous.

'You know what I want,' he said thickly. 'You want it too. You want me to stay right now and take you next door to my room. Admit it, Helen.'

'I—I can't.' She began to shake her head almost uncontrollably and he grasped it, forcing it to his shoulder, his hand like iron against her face.

'Why? I know how you feel. I'm not an immature boy.' His hard looks suddenly softened. 'I'm not Gilford either. I don't want to take you in there to beat you.'

He could have said nothing to bring her more quickly back to earth. Instantly she was struggling, panic on her face, and for a second he held her implacably.

'Tell me, Helen! Tell me what it is that makes you freeze up so completely.'

'I can't! I can't! You couldn't possibly understand.'

'Oh, I agree. If you never give me a clue then I'll be in the dark forever.' His hard voice made her cringe and he suddenly relented, easing his grip on her. 'All right. So I'm still waiting. One day, you'll tell me.'

'I won't. Not ever.'

He stood and lifted her to the bed, sitting her down like a worn-out child.

'We'll see. At least you're not crying any more. I forgot to ask you why.' He brought the dress and slid it over her head, helping her to stand until he had the zip carefully in place. 'There. A husband does have a few uses. Now we go down.'

He swung her up into his arms but she struggled, flushing when he looked down at her with wry amusement.

'I have to make my face up.'

'All right.' She was carried to the dressing-table and deposited on the stool. 'I'll come back for you.'

At the door, he paused. 'Oh—I quite forgot. The reason I came back was to tell you that we had a phone call. My mother and father have invited themselves for lunch. They'll be here in about half an hour. Donna is coming with them. I've had a word with Mrs Hill—she can make the meal stretch that far. I believe it's put her on her mettle, Americans for Christmas lunch. She's quite rosy-cheeked.'

Helen's cheeks were white. Donna here, in this house. Donna had no intention of moving far from Ross and it was clear that he accepted it happily. The magic died away, her heart returned to its normal speed. What was the use? Nothing could come of it after all.

It had the dark reality of a nightmare. Lunch was superb, a real Christmas sparkle about it that reminded Helen what a treasure she had in Mrs Hill. It was the only thing that did sparkle. Helen felt stiff with apprehension all the time, Tina was very obviously disgruntled and Ross was indifferent.

The Macleans and Donna Street had arrived with almost perfect timing, their arms filled with presents for Tansy, and Donna had breezed in, gay with laughter, her eyes sparkling at Ross. The need to give a Christmas greeting was as good an excuse as any to kiss him and Helen turned away, making a great deal of fuss over Tom Maclean and Deirdre.

'Is this putting you out?' She was over-enthusiastic in denial as Ross's father asked this question and his eyes fell to her feet as she made a move to leave the hall. 'Have you had an accident?'

'Winter games,' Ross enlightened drily. 'These athletes will overstretch themselves.'

'You've been skiing?' Donna almost pounced across to them.

'A sledge,' Helen informed her tightly.

'Oh.' She dismissed Helen and turned glowing eyes on Ross. 'Do you remember that winter when I had an accident? That awful fall at Aspen? Still, it did have its compensations—we were stuck inside for days, deliciously warm.'

Tom Maclean's eyes narrowed but Ross made no reply whatever. His arm came round Helen's slender waist, taking her weight.

'It's not a break but it's very uncomfortable. Let's get you to the table, Helen. Mrs Hill is ready to serve.'

'Don't we get a drink?' Donna pouted up at him but he ignored her coy pleading.

'Late arrivals sit down at once. This meal is too good to be kept waiting.'

'I didn't know you went in for sledging, darling.' Donna pushed in close behind as Ross helped Helen along, so close that his arm might well have been around her too.

'The sledge is a bit small for me, it's Tansy's. I only act as anchor-man.'

'You went on a child's sledge?' Donna shrieked with laughter, her tone ridiculing, and Helen's face flushed painfully. She was glad that the newly cut hair hid her face.

'She's given to bursts of great daring,' Ross commented wryly, his eyes disparaging as Helen settled in her chair. 'You never know where you are with Helen.'

'You do with me,' Donna assured him meaningly. 'I'm utterly predictable.'

'Ad nauseam,' Tom Maclean murmured as he sat close to Helen, winking at her as she gave him a startled and grateful look.

It had the effect of quieting Donna, and as Tansy and Tina took their places at the table both Ross and his father made sure that this was a happy meal for Tansy. Even Deirdre seemed to be fascinated by the little girl and Donna's nose was somewhat put out of joint.

She resumed the battle later as Ross took his parents on a tour of the house and Tina went off with Tansy after muttering to Helen that she had had 'just about enough of this do'.

Helen was settled on the long settee in the drawing-room, the coffee close by for her to serve, and Donna declined a conducted tour. She sat facing Helen in an armchair.

'You do know about Ross and me?' she enquired coolly, the claws extended now that they were alone.

'Of course. Childhood friends.'

Donna gave a contemptuous snort. 'More than that, and you'd better believe it.'

'What exactly am I supposed to believe?' Helen faced her. She had no alternative. She could sit with bowed head or face an attack head-on. This was her house, her home and anger rose inside her at the look on the other girl's face.

'I'll not give him up. I'll fight for him. *That's* what you're supposed to believe! I want Ross. I've always wanted him and this little marriage doesn't matter a damn to me.'

'You prefer other people's husbands?' Helen looked across at her with more calm than she felt. It was a direct and open challenge but she could hardly throw her out.

'I want Ross and I intend to get him. He already belongs to me. I'll get him out of this mess and back home.'

There was no time to reply. The others came back, Ross coolly enigmatic, Tom looking suspiciously at Donna and Helen's white face and Deirdre looking quite subdued.

'This is the sort of house I'll buy over here,' Tom announced, sitting at the opposite end of the settee to Helen. 'I've just been telling Ross.'

'There are quite a few on the market at present,' Ross informed him. He sat in between them, close to Helen. 'This, however, will not be for sale. This is home.'

It gave Helen a feeling of warmth and her eyes met Donna's black gaze, her own blue eyes amused. Even if Ross didn't mean it, the words must surely have given his lady-friend a nasty pang.

'Coffee?' she murmured sweetly, handing a cup across. It was taken with a barely civil nod of thanks.

'You should have that foot up,' Ross exclaimed as the coffee was all handed out and Helen sat back, not managing to suppress the slight wince as her ankle gave a nasty twinge.

'She can sit here,' Donna burst out enthusiastically, her smile returning. 'It's the obvious place, with this footstool. I'll sit by you, Ross.'

'Don't bother,' Helen said quietly. 'I can put my foot up perfectly well here.' She swung around, leaning back against the cushions and resting her long, slender legs across Ross's knee. She could fight too and she *would*. 'I'm not any great weight. Ross can stand it, I imagine.'

He had stiffened involuntarily as her leg had come across his, resting lightly against his strong thighs, but now he smiled a slow smile as he moved closer to make her comfortable.

'You're light as a feather. I seem to have been carrying you around for a long time.'

'You're accident-prone, girlie?' Tom burst into delighted laughter and Helen beamed at him. He looked like an ally to her.

'Not really. I had a migraine after we came back from Paris before Christmas. Ross carried me up to bed.'

'I bet that didn't help much.' Tom was laughing louder and Donna's face was red with annoyance.

'She went off to sleep like a lamb,' Ross informed him blandly, leaving him to make whatever he wanted of that. 'I think we'll have these sandals off,' he continued, pushing Helen's long skirt back and unfastening the straps of her silver sandals. 'Lunch being over we can relax. You've got a nicely swollen ankle there.'

'It's all right.' A burst of apprehension raced over Helen's skin now that his cool fingers were on her ankles.

'I'll decide,' he murmured softly. 'If you defy me, I'll make you stay in bed tomorrow.' His voice had dropped to seductive darkness, putting an entirely different meaning on his words, and Helen's cheeks flushed wildly, her confusion adding to Tom's amusement and Donna's fury.

Helen just had to see it through. After all, she had started all this and she could hardly slap his hands away now. He began to talk to his father and mother and Donna found herself left out of things somewhat. Helen would have been grateful to him except that his soothing fingers never left her. As he talked he began to unconsciously stroke her ankles, over the top of her foot, his fingers setting fire to her right through her body.

'Comfy?' He looked at her in a downright sensuous manner, his grey eyes sparkling like the sunlight on ice, and she nodded, swallowing hard, tearing her eyes away from his hypnotic gaze. She had started this and he wasn't about to let her forget it.

They stayed for tea. Helen wasn't quite sure that Deirdre wanted to and she was more than certain that Donna wanted to be off as fast as possible but, like his son, Tom Maclean was a very dominant character. He wanted to stay and they stayed. Helen escaped to her room for a freshen-up, Tina answering her frantic signal as she came back into the drawing-room.

'What a set of nuisances,' Tina muttered as she helped Helen upstairs.

'Tom Maclean is very nice,' Helen pointed out. 'I like him.'

'Oh, so do I. I wasn't meaning him. Your mother-in-law looks as if she's going to burst into tears and Donna Street is disgusting! She sat there almost eating Ross with her eyes. I could have died laughing when I came back in and saw him making love to your ankles. Did you see her face? She was all green and stricken.'

Well, I planned it, Helen thought. How I'm going to get out of it is the problem.

It was no problem. At bedtime, Ross carried her upstairs and deposited her on the bed, looking down at her with cool eyes when she watched him warily.

'Relax, Helen,' he drawled sardonically. 'I'm not about to spring on you and demand that you follow through. I've never had much difficulty in reading faces. I trust I played my part well?'

He walked off into his room, closing the communicating door very firmly, and she sank back on the silk sheets, miserable when she realised she was more disappointed than frightened.

CHAPTER NINE

A FEW days later, Miles came. It was quite early. Ross had not left the house because he was waiting for a telephone call from America, catching up on paperwork in the meantime. A delicate state of truce existed that Helen knew could not go on for much longer. Intensely aware of Ross as she was, her nerves were on edge and she felt he was coldly waiting for her to break. Every time their eyes accidentally met, the air seemed to catch fire. Something had to happen soon or she would be wound up to screaming-point.

Her ankle was nearly better, and she was just crossing the hall when the doorbell rang and she answered it without thought. After the days at her own cottage when she had been expecting Miles, had been angry and ready for him, she suddenly found herself facing him with no shield whatsoever. Ross had become the shield, his strength allowing her to sink back into a world where Miles was no threat, a world where only the legacy of brutality he had left could hurt her. Now she faced him alone and unprotected.

Thoughts raced desperately through her mind: how to make sure she got rid of him before Tansy came dancing down the stairs, how to stop Mrs Hill from knowing about this. Ross was locked in his study and it became terribly important that he remained there, that she could face this alone. She was ashamed to think that this man watching her should in any way touch her life with Ross. It sullied something that had become very important to her.

Her face paled and Miles stood looking at her with a cruel triumph.

'Did you expect me to just give up? Come on, now, Helen. Changing house is no way of hiding, not nowadays.'

'What do you want here?' She hardly dared do more than whisper. He stood there as he had always stood, his very presence a threat, making her stomach churn. She began to shake, and he noticed with satisfaction that brought the usual smile to his thin lips.

Oddly enough she seemed to be looking at him for the first time. She had once thought him handsome, charming. He was neither of those. His brown hair was too slick, his face beginning to fatten; even his waistline bulged a little, for all it was covered with a thick coat. She felt a wave of sickness. This man, this creature had abused her and threatened her. He was threatening now. Ross was clean and shining, a strong man in every way, his power a refuge whatever his mood. She *loved* Ross. It was all terribly clear, the comparison her mind made even under stress very obvious.

'What do you want?' Unknowingly she raised her voice, her anger climbing like a hot tide, wanting to flood him away from anything to do with Ross.

'You know what I want. I want to see my child, to get to know her before I get custody. Surely it's reasonable? She doesn't know me at all. I'll have to move in carefully, get her used to me before I take her home.'

'Get away from here or I'll call the police!' Helen's voice rose louder and he laughed, his sneer perfectly normal for him, hatefully familiar.

'And prove how unstable you are? Call the police when your ex-husband comes to see his child? They won't even answer the call. This is what they call a domestic. They don't like meddling in things like this.'

'Allow me to meddle!'

The door was pulled open wider and Ross stood there, his towering form beside her, his eyes like a frozen lake. His normal presence was daunting but now Helen thought he was the most forbidding, dangerous man she had ever seen.

'Who the hell are you?' Clearly Miles had not reckoned on meeting any male opposition.

'I'm the man who owns this house. Right at this moment you're contaminating my doorstep and attempting to intimidate my wife!'

'You've married again?' Miles stared at Helen in disbelief.

'I would say it's for the first time.' Ross looked at him ferociously and Helen knew he was in a towering rage, on the very edge of violence. Miles saw it too—he began to back away.

'One moment!' Ross moved forward, his presence so menacing that Miles stopped immediately. 'We've heard from your solicitor and we know your plans. Let me tell you ours. We'll fight you every step of the way, and money's no object.'

'You're Maclean.' Recognition suddenly seemed to dawn on Miles and his face went taut.

'I'm Maclean.' The icy grey eyes narrowed. 'And you're Gilford, owner of a computer software company that's just beginning to take off. It boils down to this: do you want to be dragged through every court, every newspaper, as you fight for a child you haven't even bothered to see in all these years? The cost would be prohibitive, in more ways than one. Maclean International would clean you out.'

'You're threatening me?' Miles was white, shaken, and Helen couldn't speak a word—not that she would have been allowed to do so. She now understood Jim's expression, 'power and drive in its raw state'.

'Oh, yes.' The very softness of his voice held its own threat.

'I can't match Maclean's.' Miles looked at Ross as if he would like to kill him but fear held him fast to the spot.

'Not in any way. We want a letter, a letter from your solicitor. The letter is to be a legal undertaking not to start any proceedings or bother my wife again. It is to be a letter that renounces any rights to a child you have not even seen. It is to give permission for the child to legally take my name. You have seven days from now.'

'And if I don't?' Two wings of red temper showed on Miles's cheeks. He was a brute and bully called to heel, thrashing about verbally when physically he dared not move.

'If you don't?' Ross gave a harsh laugh. 'That would be suicidal. Maclean's would back your competitors, your suppliers would be warned not to supply you and would be well rewarded for obedience. You've collected quite a few brains around you, people with talent. There are plenty of divisions in my firm to absorb them. We're always looking for new talent.'

'You've had me investigated!' Miles took a thoughtless step forward but Ross didn't even move. There was only the deceptively soft sound of his voice.

'Don't even think of it,' he warned. 'As to having you investigated, it took very little effort, merely a few phone calls. You're small fry. Harass my wife again however and I'll wipe—you—out.'

For a moment Miles stared at Ross, wanting to bluster, to threaten, but he saw defeat staring at him with icy eyes. 'You're welcome to the kid, and to your *wife*,' he snarled. 'It's warmer out here than it is with her. You must know her by now. She's a frigid little bitch.'

Helen shuddered and felt an arm like iron lash around her.

'One week,' Ross said with deadly quiet. 'Seven clear days and then I come after you with all the weight of the company behind me.'

'It would be different if you didn't have all your millions,' Miles blurted, his face now suffused with ugly colour.

'It would,' Ross assured him softly. 'I'd kill you now. Get off my property while you're still able to move.' He pulled Helen back and closed the door and she felt the force of his anger pulsating through the air. He simply moved away, going back to his study, and after a minute she followed.

He was packing his briefcase, his face stony, cold, his whole being unapproachable.

'You—you never told me you'd found out things about Miles.'

'You wanted to know?' His tone was quiet but acidly disparaging and he didn't bother to look up.

'It's lucky you were here.' It was a lame sort of way to thank him but he didn't look as if he would take kindly to any gushing words.

'Not luck at all,' he said flatly. 'I've had a tail on him for weeks.'

'B-before we were married?' Amazement showed on her face and he glanced across at her, a cool smile twisting his lips.

'Since our trip to Paris. I had a feeling he wouldn't just lie down for very long. After the French fiasco, I felt I owed him one.'

Helen just stared at him hopelessly and he ignored her. He snapped his case closed and picked up his jacket.

'Now I can get to work. I'll be late tonight. Don't keep dinner waiting for me. I have a date.'

She didn't need to be told who it was with.

'Thank you for being here, for protecting me—all of us,' she managed quietly and he stopped on his way out to look at her with taunting grey eyes.

'I wouldn't be much use if I couldn't protect you, would I? It's the whole point of this marriage, after all. I'm a refuge and you're a front. I think it suits us both.'

She watched him leave, saying nothing more because what was there to say? He was a refuge and he never let her down. It was a very perilous refuge, though, now that her longing to be in his arms had taken away her cold wall of safety. Loving him was strictly outside the bargain and so unexpected that she trembled whenever she thought about it.

When the threat of Miles was finally over she would have to think out her life all over again, because living close to Ross would one day prove to be too much and there was nothing she could do about her inner terror. In any case, there was Donna and there would always be Donna.

He did not come home. Helen went to bed when Tina went. She had put on a very good act. Ross had work piled sky-high—he would work until late and probably eat out. Tina accepted it; she was already studying hard for the next term that would begin the following week. It was Tansy who almost broke Helen's precarious cover of calm.

On her way to bed she turned and looked pitifully at Helen. 'Where's Daddy tonight?'

Helen just stared and then quickly picked her up and took her off to bed. 'He's working late, darling. You'll see him tomorrow.'

She tackled Tina when Tansy was safely tucked up.

'Did you tell Tansy to call Ross "Daddy"?' She was quite prepared to be furious but Tina looked at her askance.

'Give me credit for some sense, chief. When Ross wants to be called that he'll say so.'

'Then why...?'

'No great mystery. Mrs Hill thinks Ross is Tansy's father and nobody has disillusioned her. She chatters on all day to Tansy. It's obvious.'

'I—I never thought of it.' Helen looked dazed, wondering how Ross would take it when Tansy finally came out with the word in front of him. It seemed inevitable.

'Well, you've got it now and about time too,' Tina muttered, going to her own room. 'Smart kid, that,' she observed from the doorway. 'Wonder where she got her brains from? We know it can't be from Pig.'

Helen was too shattered to reply. She had never envisaged this sort of thing. She had come into this marriage imagining she could maintain her shell and now it was all stripped away. She was in love with Ross and Tansy wanted her daddy. It was a tangle that would never be unravelled.

She lay in the darkness and listened for Ross until she imagined sounds all over the house. At midnight he was still not home and she gave up then, turning her head into a pillow that was already damp with tears. He was staying all night with Donna. It was only to be expected.

The cruel hands were hurting, digging into her, bruising her skin, and she was fighting, trying not to scream. If she screamed, Tina would hear and come. He would hit Tina too.

'No! No! Let me go!' She gasped out the words, her legs kicking out. She tried to free her trapped hands but it only enraged him more, his weight becoming unbearable, making her panic further, suffocating her.

'No!' When she raised her voice, he lashed out at her, cutting into her arm, and she screamed with the sharp burst of pain, thrashing about wildly as he gripped her tightly.

'Helen! Helen! Wake up!'

It was like struggling from a deep cave of blackness and terror, the sudden voice bringing more fear, her struggles still fierce and unthinking. Her eyes refused to open and then she was being shaken.

'Helen! Open your eyes. Wake up!'

She managed it then, dragging herself back from the darkness, the light blinding her, everything swimming with the tears that streamed down her white face.

'Ross?' She looked at him in bewilderment, blinking her wild eyes but unable to stop the steady flow of tears. The communicating door was wide open right back to the wall and Ross was sitting beside her, his hands on her arms tight and burning.

'You were having a nightmare. I heard you struggling and muttering and I was halfway in here before that horrifying scream.' He let her go and ran his hand through the thick darkness of his hair. 'I thought you were being raped!'

She bit down on her lips to stop the tears, thankful he wasn't looking at her. 'I—I was dreaming.'

'That's a grave understatement.' He looked at her wryly and she began to focus properly. He was in a dark silk dressing-gown, his feet bare, and his hair looked curiously ruffled as if he had been running his hands through it for hours. It was the first time she had seen him undressed and she looked away quickly, avoiding his vividly grey eyes.

'If you're all right, I'll go.' His voice was back to coldness as he stood up, preparing to leave her alone. 'Would you like a drink?'

'Yes. I—I'm going to get up and have a cup of tea. I have to walk about and—and...'

'Get your act together? Where's your robe?' He spotted it on a chair and reached for it. 'Come on. After that I think I need something too, a mite stronger than tea. I'll go down with you.'

He stood waiting and she had to get out of bed to slip into her robe. She turned as he held it out for her. She was still shaking and dazed from her nightmare, too grateful for his presence to feel any qualms, and the fact that her nightie was all but transparent, the straps little more than ribbons, didn't seem to penetrate her mind.

'What's this?' Ross stopped with her robe only halfway on to her shoulders, his finger tracing the small deep scar that ran along the top of her arm. Such had been the power of the dream that Helen winced as if she still felt the pain. 'It looks healed. Does it hurt?'

'No. Of—of course not. It's old.'

'Then why did you wince like that?'

He turned her round when she made no answer, his eyes intently on her.

'Was that part of the dream? Did Gilford do that?'

Helen hung her head, struggling into her robe, tying it tightly around her tiny waist—she could not meet his eyes, grey and probing.

'Helen?'

The tone told her he was not about to be fobbed off with anything less than the truth, and she took a shaky breath.

'It was a ring. He has a ring on his right hand, a—a flashy sort of thing with stones. It's a very elaborate setting, quite sharp.'

'And?' His hands had come back to her shoulders, tightening when she stopped explaining.

'The ring caught me. I—I expect it was an accident.'

'An accident?' He tilted her face and she had to look at the white fury on his. 'He was hitting you. That's what the nightmare was about. What did he use, the back of his hand or his fist?'

'His fist,' she whispered, the shaking beginning again as she relived her dream and the whole nightmare of the past reality. 'I only screamed when the ring hurt so much because—because Tina would have come, you see, and— he might have...' Tears began to stream down her face again and he pulled her tightly into his arms.

'Why didn't I kill the bastard when I had him here this morning?' he grated. 'I'll find him and——!'

'No! No, Ross, please!' She was so shaken by her revelations and by his fury that she clutched him without thought, her arms tightening around his waist as he held her close. 'It was a long time ago. I just want safety for Tansy. I don't want to even think about Miles.'

She buried her face against his chest, her tears flooding freely, but he lifted her chin, his other arm holding her fast.

'But you *do* think about him! He even sneaks into your dreams, frightening you, torturing you. Do you think I'm letting him get away with it?'

'Please, Ross!' She looked up at him with unhappy blue eyes, her lashes starred with tears, and he frowned down at her, his clear grey eyes filled with frustration.

'You leave me helpless—you know that? I can't act as I wish, protect you as I wish because none of this is real. I may be legally married to you but I've left you with the right to call all the tunes, even when it's with Gilford. For heaven's sake, Helen! I wouldn't do that with any other woman!'

Helen could only look at him, her cheeks glittering with tears, and he glared down at her before murmuring frustratedly, cupping her head tightly and covering her mouth with his.

It was no gentle kiss. Every bit of his anger and frustration was in it, bringing a cruelty to his mouth that had not been there when he had kissed her before. Even so, it brought a feeling of calm, a feeling of belonging, his touch driving the nightmare far away, right out of her mind. Instantly aroused, she melted, moving closer, and her movement seemed to bring him to his senses.

His dark head lifted and he eased her away, not releasing her but giving her the opportunity to move from him.

'I'm sorry, Helen. I'm sorry,' he muttered hoarsely. 'Heaven only knows you've suffered enough brutality without any more.' He looked at her ruefully but she stared back entranced, her lips softened and swollen, her eyes closing as she swayed right into his arms.

'Helen?' He caught her closer and whispered her name. 'Helen?'

She couldn't speak at all. She was even afraid of her own actions but her fingers tightened on his robe, clutching him closer, accepting his kiss hungrily when he took her lips.

In seconds they were utterly lost to the world, seeking each other greedily, Helen kissing him back as wildly as she could, clutching him to her with all her strength, her arms wrapped around his neck as he arched her back, his lips trailing over her throat, nuzzling the rounded swell of her breasts above the lacy-topped satin of her nightie. He was taking in the scent of her, his breathing heavy and erratic, his body alert, attuned to each small sound she made, each little moan of pleasure.

His mouth came back to hers, nipping and caressing until she felt faint with excitement.

'I can't let you go, not this time. I want you, Helen. I want you too badly to let you go!' The words were breathed into her mouth and the old fear rose but her body was pressed to his, his taut thighs moving against her, and when his hand slid down her back to mould her to his throbbing desire, fear flew away, her body unaware of her mind's warning. All she knew now was the feeling he generated inside her, this aching to be submerged in him.

She moved her hips against his, her breathing a pleading gasp, and his hands stripped off her robe with feverish need, his lips fused with hers. Cool air washed over her heated skin as the nightie was pushed from her shoulders to slide unchecked to the floor. Far from frightening her it brought her back to him with a rush of emotion, her arms clinging tightly.

'Helen! You're so soft...so beautiful...I've wanted to touch you for such a very long time, to hold you like this.' His tongue teased her lips and then moved into her mouth, searching the sweetness urgently. His hand found her breast, his fingers caressing the hard nipple until she shook in his arms, gasping with need.

She was completely out of control, mindless with the delight of his touch, a trembling, yearning creature his arms had to subdue, her breath gasping in her throat, muffled little cries escaping to drive him to the end of endurance.

'Yes, darling, yes. It's all right.'

His voice was thickened beyond recognition and even when he lifted her and placed her on the bed she clung to him, overwhelmed, captivated, her body fretful to be close as he eased fractionally away to shrug out of his robe.

'I'm not leaving you, Helen. I'm not leaving you,' he whispered hoarsely. His arms enclosed her again, gripping her tightly. 'Come here to me.'

She was torn between two worlds, her body craving his, moving of its own volition back to him, shuddering at the feel of his skin against hers. But her mind fought, stiffened, warned her. She couldn't do this. She was frozen, incapable, frigid. A sob welled up in her throat, an agonising sound as she felt her body stiffen too, fear winning so easily. She turned her face away and Ross lifted his head, disbelief in his voice.

'Helen! Don't leave me now! We want each other. It's beautiful.'

'I can't! I can't!' The words seemed to be dragged out of her from some deep core of loneliness, and his brief anger faded as he heard her voice.

'You're crying! Have I hurt you? Am I frightening you? Look at me, please!' She shook her head, keeping her eyes tightly closed, shame washing across the whole of her body.

'I—I can't go any further. I'm so sorry, Ross. This is all my fault.'

'A minute ago you wanted me,' he said huskily. 'A minute ago you were the most wild and passionate woman I've ever held in my arms. You wanted me in any way you could get me, just as I want you.'

'I thought I did. I was so *sure*, but I know now I can't. I can never... I'm frigid, Ross. Agreeing to the sort of marriage you wanted was easy for me because I'm completely cold.'

'Cold?' Astonishingly his hand stroked her face, gentle although his fingers trembled. 'Are you? Who told you that—Gilford?'

'Yes. But I knew anyway. I never wanted him to touch me. I never let him close—like—like this and when we were married... I—I couldn't! It was hateful. It disgusted me.'

'And he forced you.'

'Yes.' Tears streamed down her face, shame overwhelming her. She would never be able to face him again, now that he knew her total degradation.

His hands cupped her face and she felt the deep stillness in him that came before his anger, so that when he spoke so softly she was bewildered, shocked into opening her eyes.

'Yes,' he said quietly. 'Look at me, Helen. Admit where you are. Are you disgusted now? Is it hateful to be lying naked in my arms?'

'No.' She shook her head, apprehension in her blue eyes. 'But you see, I can't...'

'I told you a long time ago that I'd never ask anything you weren't capable of. I still won't. Just relax, stop being afraid. Let me hold you. I need to. Have I ever hurt you?'

She shook her head, her eyes held by his as she slowly subsided, her fear draining away a little at a time, her stiff body, so cold and taut, beginning to warm against his skin.

'Oh, Helen.' He smiled down at her, his face gentle. 'How can you believe you're cold, frigid? What does that mean, for pity's sake? Almost from the first I could look at you and make your legs shake. A few minutes ago I was going out of my mind to be inside you, where you wanted me to be. Yes, you can blush,' he taunted softly as a faint colour flooded over her skin. 'Did that disgust you? Can't you bear to hear things like that? What if I tell you that I've wanted you right where you are now for weeks, ever since Paris—before Paris?' His fingers traced around her nipple, exciting it back to life. 'I wanted to do so many things to you. This, and this.' His dark head bent and gently he took the aching peak into his mouth, tugging until she murmured in agitation and arched against him desperately.

'Helen,' he murmured, moving closer, accepting the way her hips rose to him. 'There are no frigid women, just damned bad lovers. Trust me, darling,' he whispered against her mouth. 'Nothing, but nothing is going to hurt you.'

He kissed her tears away, his lips moving over her cheeks, over her neck, his tongue tracing the trembling line of her jaw.

'Don't you know what a volatile mixture you are, how you make me feel? Black hair, blue eyes, the mixture of fear and defiance. I want to devour you over and over with no pause for breath and each time will be better than the last.' He gave a low sensuous laugh, his breath exciting her skin. 'You're not cold, Helen. You're burning me up. I only have to look at you to want to be here.'

Fire stared deep inside her, his seductive words arousing her as much as his skilful hands, the kisses he placed on her heated skin bringing back the small wild sound to her throat. It was true. She didn't have to hide inside, not with Ross.

She clung to him, trembling and aware, murmuring his name, a brilliant flame inside burning her to heated life, hungry life. Her hands slid over his shoulders, glorying in the feel of his skin, urging him closer.

'Not until you're ready,' he murmured thickly, his head lowered as he began to kiss every part of her. 'I have to kiss you here and here.'

He clasped her tightly when she twisted wildly against him, holding her and caressing her until her nails were digging into his brown shoulders, her body struggling to get closer, demanding and wild.

Even when he parted her thighs the desperation raged inside her, no sign of the cold fear that had been her nightmare for so long.

'Only what you want to give, Helen,' he whispered against her lips as he moved her beneath him. He seemed to be waiting, almost weightless above her, holding back the fulfilment she now so desperately wanted, and she cried out in frustration.

'Ross! Don't stop! Please don't stop! Ross!'

She gasped as he entered her, pain coming for one brief second, and then she closed silkily around him, moving with him, her breathing fast and wild, her hands clutching him urgently, her body moving to the same rhythm, his name on her lips frenziedly.

'Now, darling! Now!' His voice was hoarse with passion and they rocketed off the world together as Helen spun into colours and light that were fulfilment, her body floating with Ross somewhere way above the night, her own cries of delight mingling with the flutter of a thousand wings.

It took a long time to come back because there was a new kind of reality. There was the joy of release, the power of his arms, the feel of his lips trailing against her hot cheeks.

'Well?' He lay above her, his hand tilting her chin, and she opened bewildered eyes.

'I feel faint.' She looked at him with wonder in her eyes and he laughed softly, his breathing not yet quite normal.

'Join the club. I couldn't move if I tried. I've a horrible suspicion I may never be able to move again.'

His lips traced hers when she looked at him with wildly flushed cheeks, her eyes just a little anxious.

'Don't ask me how you were, woman. You've knocked me sideways.' He took her head in two strong hands, shaking it gently. 'And don't ask me to leave you alone ever again. I can't. You've been forbidden fruit for far too long. From this night forward, we're married.'

'I've never before... I mean...'

'I know.' He moved to lay facing her, lifting her into the curve of his arm. For a few moments they lay closely together not speaking and she knew he was letting her grow calm, letting her relive the moments and the wonder. She was alive again, alive for the first time since her parents had died.

Suddenly she wanted to tell Ross how she felt, to confess her love, even if he felt nothing but desire. She turned to him, lifting her hand to touch him, but he caught it in his strong fingers, holding it fast.

'Tell me about Gilford,' he said, no sign of passion left in his voice, just the same relentless determination she had come to know so well.

'You know.' She wanted to move now, to twist away, to pull her hand from his, but he would not allow it.

'Some things you've told me, some I've pieced together, but there's more, Helen. He bullied you, made you help him in a way that was anathema to someone as shy and sensitive as you. He beat you in bed and out of it. And yet you stayed. I can understand partly. I can understand your not wanting anyone to know. I can understand that you wanted help when you were alone, with Tina to take care of and you not much more than a girl yourself. And I can understand your being too frightened to leave. What happened to finally make you leave? Where did that courage come from?'

'It was over a long time ago,' Helen whispered. She was perfectly still, all the joy dying out of her.

'It will never be over until you tell me.' He moved, leaning over her, looking down into her face. 'Tonight we've almost freed you. Take the last step, take it with me.'

Was that what it had all been about? To free her? She closed her eyes, too ashamed to face him as she spoke.

'It was what he said.' There was no tone to her voice, only a small thread of sound that had his eyes narrowing. 'It was the night—the night I got the scar. He called me all the things he was so used to calling me. Until then I'd taken it and said nothing.' She gave a funny little laugh. 'I believed him anyway. He just looked down at me as if I were nothing and he said—he said that Tina was more of a woman. He said she was growing into a very interesting girl and that he would see how she liked him next night.'

'What did you do?' When she looked up at Ross, his face was white, his mouth edged with fury.

'I fought him. I scratched and bit and screamed. I pulled his hair and hurt him. That was when he hit me and got really violent. I couldn't do anything then. I was trapped. He was lying on top of me with his hands round my throat, shaking me and shouting. Tina thought he was going to kill me.'

'Tina?'

'She had heard me scream and she came in. She had a pretty good idea of what was going on but I'd never admitted it. I'd never screamed before, though. I don't know how long she'd been standing there but she certainly heard the last part and she could see the terror I was in. There was a big vase. Before I knew she was there she was hitting him with it. She just let her temper take over. She didn't stop. I had to pull her away finally. For a minute I thought she'd killed him.'

He stroked her face gently, seeing the agitation that was still there as she lived it all again.

'Then what?' he asked quietly.

'He was all right. People like Miles are always all right. He was too groggy to retaliate though and we crept away and made our plans. When it was light, we left. After that I didn't see him except with my solicitor and I never told all the truth. I agreed to an amicable arrangement because I didn't want Tina mentioned or anything like that. If I hadn't agreed we wouldn't have him coming here now.'

'He won't come again,' Ross assured her tightly. 'I can promise you that.' He pulled her into his arms. 'I know it took a lot of courage to tell me that, but it's all over. Now you're better, no secrets between us. No worries or hurts.'

None except Donna, none except the fact that he didn't love her as she loved him, but in an odd sort of way she was happy. She smiled and felt him relax, the tight temper draining away.

'From now on you can forget him. A man like that is totally inadequate and cruelty gives him some sort of status in his own mind. Men like Gilford are emotional cripples. They can't care for people. They don't even *like* women. Forget him, Helen, all he will ever do is hurt and hurt. All your wounds will heal; he's like that for life.' He pulled her against him as he turned, settling her in his arms. 'Go to sleep. Do you know it's three o'clock?'

'Are you staying here?' she asked quietly, wanting him to with an urgency that shook her.

'Am I welcome?'

'Yes.'

He tightened his arms around her and in a few moments he was fast asleep. He had called her darling, so many times, been passionate and gentle. If that was all there would ever be she was more blessed than many other women. She loved him deeply, his sleeping face, relaxed and calm, the dearest thing she could think of.

CHAPTER TEN

IN THE morning Ross had left before Helen awoke. For a long time she lay in bed, reliving the previous night, her pulses racing. There was the imprint of his head against the pillow to assure her that that it had not been some wild erotic dream, and as she showered and dressed she realised that she didn't even want to leave this room, this place where happiness had been given back to her. His name was ringing round in her head like the chimes of a shining bell. It was impossible to keep the smile from her face.

There had been a heavy fall of snow in the night and when she went down to breakfast she found Tina already there, Tansy at the window, watching the snow with excited eyes.

'We can sledge again,' Helen said cheerfully, feeling about sixteen and looking it had she but known.

'Sorry, chief. No sledging. Orders from the boss. At least, as I recall we can go out *with* the sledge but we're not to take it on the hill unless he's here. He reminded me rather forcefully of your twisted ankle.' She glanced at Helen out of her eye corners. 'What does it feel like to be wrapped in cotton wool?' She grinned as Helen blushed brightly. 'Aha! I believe I have you at a disadvantage.'

'Let's build a snowman!' Helen said with breathless enthusiasm, turning to Tansy to hide from her sister's knowing expression.

'I've got some big old buttons that will do nicely for eyes,' Mrs Hill promised, coming in with Helen's breakfast. She beamed at Helen. 'This is such a lovely, happy house, Mrs Maclean. My own little quarters are so snug and warm. It's nice to have my own furniture around me after so long in other people's rooms. I expect that little addition to the house was meant to be a Granny flat?'

'I think it probably was, Mrs Hill.' Helen smiled. 'I'm glad you're happy here and like the annex. We don't have a granny.'

'Well, there's Deirdre,' Tina mused wryly as Mrs Hill went happily away. 'As grannies go, however, she's sadly lacking. Hope she's securely back in New York by now.'

'I feel a bit sorry for her,' Helen said quietly. She felt a bit sorry for herself too when she thought of Donna but she pulled herself up quickly. 'Let's get to that snowman,' she reminded them.

It took all morning, and by the time they came in for lunch they all had rosy cheeks and a giant snowman stood in front of the house, shiny blue buttons for eyes, coal for the nose and an old cap and scarf belonging to Tina to keep him warm. Tansy was almost frantic with joy, happier than Helen had ever seen her, so relaxed and carefree in this house.

They curled up by the fire and Helen found herself glancing frequently at her watch, her cheeks brighter than ever when she realised she was counting the hours to Ross's coming home. A few days ago she had been so frightened and now she was wanting to be in his arms with a longing that made her tremble.

The sound of a car just before teatime had her running to the window. It was half-past three, not yet dark at all, and she felt her heart sink as a fast sports car drew up in front of the house. Deirdre Maclean got out, wrapped in furs, as smart and glossy as ever, but it was the driver who held Helen's dismayed glance. Donna

Street was here without invitation and looking smugly pleased with herself.

'Oh, my hat!' Tina stood beside Helen at the window and then turned quickly, gathering up her things and Tansy's. 'I'm sorry, chief. I can't face those two, you're on your own. Tell them that Tansy is in the nursery with her nanny and, if they want to come up, we've got measles.'

Even before the bell rang she was on her way upstairs, Tansy clutched against her, and Helen went across the hall alone to face them, her heart sinking. It could only mean trouble and she was not yet secure enough with Ross to face that.

'Oh, Helen. You look so colourful.' Deirdre forced a smile at the sight of Helen in her jeans and bright red sweater. 'All that blue-black hair. It's quite astonishing really.'

Obviously she was talking to summon up courage for something, and Helen led them to the drawing-room. Donna hadn't thought it necessary to even say hello.

'You're just in time for tea,' Helen managed calmly, ringing for Mrs Hill.

'Yes. Tea. Of course, the English take afternoon tea, don't they?' Deirdre murmured distractedly. 'I—I wanted to talk to you, Helen. That's why I'm here.'

'That's why we're both here,' Donna put in with a wintry smile.

Helen ignored her. 'What can I do for you?' she asked Deirdre when Mrs Hill had left the room.

'I want you to persuade Ross to go back to New York.' Deirdre's words tumbled out in a rush. 'He's not going to be happy in this little place for very long, Helen, and it means a lot to me. If Ross goes back to the States then Tom will give up the idea of moving over to England permanently.'

'Ross seems to like it here,' Helen began, but Donna chipped in ruthlessly.

'Novelty! That's what all of this is, simply novelty. He'll go back home finally because I just can't hang around her indefinitely and when I go, of course, Ross will follow. We've never been separated for long so it's only a matter of time and, in the meantime, Deirdre is unhappy. You should think about that.'

Some of the lovely colour faded from Helen's face. Well, this was certainly laying it on the line, and Deirdre hadn't said a word of contradiction. Helen felt anger rising swiftly. She would fight for Ross, but she could only fight if he wanted her enough.

'Ross will do exactly as he likes,' she said as calmly as possible.

'He certainly will.' The deep, dark voice from the doorway had them all jumping guiltily, and Helen sprang to her feet feeling a wave of agitation as she saw Ross standing just inside the room, his eyes glittering as he took in the scene. None of them had heard him arrive. As usual he just seemed to appear when she needed him, but she had no real idea of his feelings. Wanting her was not enough to keep him here if he loved Donna.

His power silenced them all and then he was walking across the room, his eyes on Helen, running over her from her black shining hair to her suddenly pale face.

'So you built a snowman without me?' he taunted softly, his arm coming around her slender waist. 'I don't like being left out. Later there'll be punishment.' He could feel her trembling and he drew her closer, tucking her against his shoulder and turning to face the visitors.

He ignored Donna, his eyes impatiently on his mother.

'We're off again, are we?' he rasped, the indulgent teasing immediately gone from his voice. 'Let's get one thing straight right now. I live here and I'm staying here and that's permanent. If I go to New York it will be for a visit only and my family will go too. Dad and I have had this move planned for a very long time. He wants to come home, back to England, and I reckon it's about time he had some happiness.' He glared at his mother. 'He *loves* you! All these years of pointless jealousy. If he finally takes up with another woman I wouldn't blame him in the least. Why he's put up with your insane jealousy for so long I'll never know.'

'Ross!' Deirdre looked at him pitifully but he was totally unmoved.

'What? You think I shouldn't speak about this in front of Helen? Helen is my wife. We don't have secrets. You had the nerve to come here and try to pressurise her and that gives me *carte blanche*. Get it fixed in your mind that *nothing* will get me back to New York permanently. Dad will come here and if you've any sense, any feeling for a man who loves you, you'll come too.'

'You don't know your father——'

'Don't know him? I've worked with him for years, seen him miserable and lonely, listened to him over drinks in some bar while you've been entertaining and telling yourself he was out with another woman. More often than not he was out with me. *You* don't know him, and if you continue like this for much longer you'll lose him.'

Deirdre started to cry and Donna looked at Ross angrily.

'Now look! You shouldn't speak to her like that.' Her face suddenly softened as she saw his dangerous looks. 'I understand, though. You're all upset, undecided. It doesn't matter, you don't have to rush into anything. I'll be staying in England.'

'It's a free country,' Ross commented sardonically. He looked across at his mother and then moved to pull her to her feet. 'I know it's been hell,' he said quietly, 'but it's been hell for Dad too and there's no reason for it. Go upstairs with Helen and pull yourself together a bit.'

She nodded, giving Helen a rather shaken glance. 'If I could powder my nose?'

'Of course.' Helen put her arm around Deirdre's shoulders. She could see the same sort of tight misery in this woman that she had felt herself—illogical, tearing emotion. Helen's kind heart went out to her, to Tom Maclean too.

In the bedroom, Deirdre looked at Helen with anxious eyes, so at variance with her normal appearance that Helen could see how deeply this went.

'Do you think Ross is telling me the truth, about Tom, I mean?'

'Have you ever known Ross lie?' Helen asked simply.

'No, never.' She turned to the dressing-table and touched her hair anxiously. 'I'm feeling old, you see, Helen. When I was young, I was such a beauty. Tom was wild about me. For years now I've tried to keep it up, to glitter, to look younger.'

'You do look young,' Helen said quietly, going to lean against the dressing-table and looking down at her, her eyes full of pity. 'When I first saw you, I thought how very beautiful you were. Maybe Tom doesn't want you to glitter if it means he sees less of you. Maybe he wants to come here because New York is too fast, too hard. You could be together a lot more in England, relax, start all over again, visit Paris, Rome, Madrid.'

'Do you think so?' Deirdre looked at her with hopeful eyes and Helen smiled down at her.

'I don't think you really feel old. I think you probably feel tired with all that endless entertaining, all that pointless worrying. You'll feel better a long way from it. Go back and tell Tom.'

'Oh, Helen! I will!' She stood up and gave Helen a hug, a real one this time. 'When you have children we'll be near.'

'I'd like that,' Helen said truthfully. 'You can't stay in the granny flat, though,' she added with a grin.

'Granny! Don't start me off again.' Deirdre looked at herself in the mirror and touched her hair, evidently more pleased now with what she saw. 'Can you phone me a taxi, Helen, and check for a train? I can't wait for Donna. It will take hours for her to drive back to London and I want to see Tom.'

'I'll do it now,' Helen said firmly, turning to the phone, and Deirdre touched her arm.

'Don't take any notice of Donna, Helen,' she begged.

'I won't.' Not if Ross cares, even if he only cares a little bit.

The taxi was already on its way when they went downstairs, and whatever Donna had wanted to say had remained unsaid because Tina was there with Tansy and Ross was absorbed with them. Whether Tina had come down deliberately or not Helen didn't know, but she listened with thoughtful eyes as Deirdre told Ross that she was going back by train at once, and he smiled and he saw her more hopeful look.

'Snap out of it,' he advised, and she gave him a little smile.

'I'm going to.' She said goodbye to Tansy too as Tina made to take her back up the stairs.

'I'll see you soon,' she promised, kissing the soft little cheek. 'Next time, your grandfather will come too.'

If Tina was startled by this turn of events she said nothing, but her looks spoke volumes as she went up the stairs with Tansy's hand firmly in her own.

'I'm staying,' Donna announced, and Deirdre looked at her anxiously and then at Ross. All he did was shrug and Helen felt the same old sick feeling surging back. She took Deirdre to the door to see her off as the taxi came, and she walked right out with her to see her into the taxi, stopping for another word of encouragement. She didn't want to face the drawing-room with Ross and Donna alone in there and her steps were slow as she came back. She closed the front door softly and stood there for a minute to gather her courage.

'I'm not leaving you, Ross. I'm not letting you go.' She heard Donna's voice vibrantly sincere and Helen bit into her lip, waiting for the reply. It was impatient, like the sound of a man who had heard quite enough nonsense.

'Do yourself a favour, Donna—grow up!' he snapped. 'If you need drama, join a group.'

'You've always cared about me!' There was a rather frantic sound to her voice now and Ross snorted angrily.

'You've spent years throwing yourself at me, you mean,' he rasped. 'When you were a teenager it was amusing. It stopped being amusing years ago. Take my advice, Donna, find yourself a man who wants you before it's too late. I don't want you, heaven knows,' he added wearily.

'You *did* want me!'

'Well, if I did, I never noticed. If I did, I've had plenty of opportunity to take action. You were an amusing teenager who grew into a pest. Stay in England if you like, follow me around, but all you'll do is hurt yourself.'

'You're staying with her?'

'Yes, I'm staying with Helen,' he grated impatiently. 'I *love* her!' His voice softened. 'In fact that's hardly the way to describe it. I'm mad about her, crazy about her. I can't bear to let her out of my sight.'

'She's not like us. You'll get tired of her!' She sounded on the edge of hysteria but Ross didn't seem to notice. He made a strange little sound in his throat.

'Tired of her? Maybe. When I get tired of breathing, tired of being alive. She's everything I'll ever want. I've looked for her all my life. You see this ring on my finger? Helen put it there. It means—forever.'

Helen suddenly realised that she was still standing there, leaning against the front door, tears streaming down her face, and she hastily wiped them away with trembling fingers. He loved her—her eyes were dreamy with happiness and she took several deep breaths before she joined them both.

'Did you see her safely off?' Ross looked across at her as she came in, his eyes alert at once at the sign of tears on her lashes.

'Yes. She'll be all right. She promised to phone as soon as she got back. It's snowing again,' she added, glancing at Donna. This woman who sat so sullenly in the chair by the fire was no threat to her now, but she still didn't want to have to offer her a room for the night.

Mrs Hill popped her head round the door and smiled at them.

'Will there be extra people for dinner, Mrs Maclean?' she asked Helen, but Rose answered before Helen could speak.

'No, Mrs Hill, just the family. Miss Street can't make her mind up whether she's driving back to London or staying the night at the White Bear. Either way, she won't be here for dinner.'

'Thank you, sir.' As Mrs Hill closed the door, Donna got up and gathered her bag. She didn't look at either of them. She simply swept out. It was the only way that Helen could describe it and she blinked her eyes as the front door slammed. She dared not look at Ross.

'Have a good journey,' he murmured, laughter at the back of his voice, and she looked up then, meeting laughing grey eyes, no sign of ice about them at all. There was no time to speak. Tina came in, glancing around theatrically.

'Coast clear?' she asked wryly.

'Completely,' Ross assured her.

'Are we dressing for dinner?' Tina wanted to know and Ross sighed heavily.

'Just give me peace, ladies, that's all I ask.'

Tansy ran to him and not to Helen and he scooped her up in his arms, hugging her.

'Can I stay up for dinner tonight, Daddy?' she wheedled.

'You certainly can,' he said softly. He sounded perfectly normal but Helen could see his face and knew the pleasure that one word had given him. Her eyes met Tina's satisfied glance. 'I'll take you up to bed afterwards,' Ross added. 'You can have a piggy-back, a shoulder-ride or a carry.'

'I'll have a carry,' Tansy decided, thinking it out quickly.

'That's settled, then,' Ross said. 'Now, about this snowman...'

After dinner, as the evening drew to a close, Ross sat back on the settee, pulling Helen down beside him, his arms wrapping around her. They had not had a minute alone and he sighed, his head resting back.

'They say nothing ever happens in the country,' he mused ruefully. 'I find it hard to get a minute's peace.'

'Why are you back so early?' Helen asked softly, leaning against him, loving every minute of his nearness.

'Dad phoned. He warned me that an expedition had set out in this direction.' He looked down at her gently.

'I wasn't sure that you were quite up to dealing with it yet.'

'Donna—alarmed me,' she confessed quietly.

'Me too.' He gave a harsh laugh. 'She's been under my feet for so long that I'd got to the stage when I didn't even notice her. When someone's been flinging themselves into your arms since she was a child you get blind to it. I only began to realise what a pest she really was when they came over this time. She was bent on trouble, like all children when their toys are removed.'

'Were you a toy?' Helen asked quietly and he looked down at her with questioning eyes.

'A ridiculous fixation. Are you jealous?' There was just the underlying sound of anxiety there and Helen laughed up at him, her blue eyes sparkling.

'Not after I heard what you said to her.'

'Eavesdropping?' His dark brows rose, his eyes glittering down at her. 'I trust you enjoyed it?'

'Yes.' Her face flushed but she went on looking at him. 'Don't be angry.'

'I'm trying to be,' he warned her softly. 'Somehow or other, though, I can't.' His arms tightened as he watched her bewitching face, her dancing blue eyes, the way her black hair swung around her face. 'You're beautiful,' he said huskily.

Tina came into the room then, stopping any further moves on his part. She came straight to the point as usual.

'It's New Year's Eve,' she reminded them briskly. 'I suppose we'll have to stay up and see it in? I don't mind that but I'm not singing "Auld Lang Syne." I feel so utterly stupid doing that.'

Ross began to laugh and she looked at him haughtily.

'I mean it! I'm prepare to open the door and let the Lucky Bird in but that's it.'

Helen got up and stretched sleepily. 'If you want to whistle at the open door, just go ahead,' she suggested. 'As for me, I'm going to bed. Anyway, I'm scared if I open the door the Lucky Bird might just get out.'

'Good! My sentiments exactly,' Tina announced, making for the door, then she stopped to frown at Ross mockingly. 'It's no use your staying up either. Americans don't know about our strange rituals.'

'You'd be surprised,' he laughed. He turned to Helen when the door had closed. 'Come on,' he urged. 'Speaking of rituals, I've got something to show you.'

When the lights had been put out, they walked upstairs, Ross with his arm around Helen, and she ventured a question that had been right there in her mind for days.

'Your mother and father—will they be all right?'

'I surely hope so. She's been like this for years. If I were in his place, I'd be demented.'

'She feels that she's getting old, Ross,' Helen said softly. 'She thinks he doesn't want her in the same way. She told me he used to be wild about her.'

'He still is!' Ross looked down at her in amazement. 'You mean she told you this in those few minutes upstairs? Hell! We've been trying to find out what was wrong for years. We even had a psychiatrist lined up at one time but she wouldn't see him.'

'It's hardly surprising,' Helen pointed out drily. 'Obviously she was afraid he would tell her she was looking old and that it happened to everyone.'

'And what did you tell her, my cunning little wife?'

'I told her she was beautiful. I told her she was probably just tired with worry and too many parties. I pointed out that England is more tranquil than New York. She's gone back to discuss a future move in this direction.'

'You're a miracle,' he said softly, his arm tightening. 'Let's forget them now. I told you I had something to show you.'

Upstairs he led her through her own room and into his, his eyes amused at her mystified expression.

'What is it?' She looked round, seeing nothing at all, and he pointed to his bed.

'It's a bed. I'll give you two seconds to get into it.'

His eyes were alive with laughter and, when she blushed to a rosy hue, he caught her close, kissing her flushed cheeks.

'Am I frightening you?'

'No. I'm just shocked at your chauvinistic way of speaking.' She was laughing too and shivering against him, so happy that she could hardly speak at all.

'I don't know any better,' he breathed against her neck. 'Come and show me how to behave.'

Unable to keep away from him, her arms went round his waist, but he suddenly drew back, teasing gone, his face entreating.

'Tell me, Helen! Tell me,' he begged.

'I love you,' she whispered, knowing exactly what he wanted to hear. 'When I first saw you, something happened inside that I'd never felt before. I didn't know what it was and it just grew and grew. I felt frightened, excited, shaken. I know now what it was. I was falling in love, right from the first.'

'Oh, darling, darling.' He rocked her in his arms, holding her tightly. 'You don't know what you did to me. A black-haired witch with blue eyes and a lovely bewildered face. You went from frigid, to anger, to shyness with such alarming rapidity that I couldn't keep up with the sensations that raced through me. I wanted you so much it was agony. At first, I thought you had some man hidden away, somebody so special that you were prepared to risk your job to go to him early each night.'

'And you were disgusted when you thought I was unmarried, with a child,' she reminded him softly.

'Disgusted? How could I be disgusted with you?' he asked with such a shocked look that she had to believe him. 'No, sweet. I was just devastated. I wanted you to belong to me and only me. I couldn't face the thought of any other man having been in your life. It hurt! Even so early I knew there was you and nobody else. I had a sleepless night—several sleepless nights.'

'What made you change your mind?' Helen asked, looking into his eyes.

'You did. Your frightened little face, your bewildered, hurt eyes. The fact that I loved you.'

'And in Paris I shocked you all over again.'

'Yes,' he confessed. 'I couldn't believe it, my fastidious Helen letting those men paw her. I could have killed them right there and then. I was in a wild rage and just added to your fright.'

'No. Not really.' Her hand came gently to his mouth, her fingers tracing his lips. 'It was the beginning for me. I cared what you thought. I saw the fury on your face when you knew what I'd had to do. It was the first part of the healing.'

'And last night?' he asked huskily.

'I came back to life.' She threw her arms around his neck. 'Oh, Ross, I love you so much. When I saw Donna today...'

'I have never, *ever* made love to her,' he assured her seriously. 'I never even thought of it. She was just a kid who was pushed under my nose by my mother and after that she grew up into an almighty pest.'

'You kissed her at the reception,' Helen reminded him. 'And I—I saw you putting her into a taxi, that day in London.'

'I wondered what was wrong.' He lifted her face, his hands cupping it warmly. 'Donna was kissing me. With her it's a habit—now broken,' he added determinedly. 'She got the reaction one would get from kissing a piece of wood. All I wanted was to get to you, on both occasions. Believe me?'

'Yes. So you didn't want to marry me to get away from her?'

'I wanted to marry you to get you for myself,' he assured her. 'Offering you a bargain was the only way you were going to agree. I prayed that when you were safe and close to me you would want me. You did.'

'I did,' she agreed, 'so much.'

She smiled up into his eyes and his face softened, his smile growing.

'About the bed,' he reminded her. 'You're making no attempt to get ready. Is this your idea of efficiency? If you worked for me, I'd fire you.'

Helen clung to him as he took over the job himself, sliding the bright red sweater over her head, stopping to look at her as she stood before him, naked to the waist.

'Does this bother you?' he asked as he looked down at her.

'Only because I'm shy still,' she whispered.

'I don't mind that at all.' His hands stroked her breasts. 'You're beautiful.' His voice was thickened and her breathing changed to match the rhythm of her heart, fast, racing, erratic.

'Ross!' She moved right into his arms and he lifted her at once, cradling her against him.

'I know,' he murmured against her lips. 'I've missed you all day, darling, so much. Can we wait any longer?'

Helen shook her head, too filled with emotion to speak, and he carried her to bed, his bed where she would always be from this moment on.

When they were lying close together, the silence only broken by the sound of their urgent breathing, she was swept back into the bliss of the night before, waves of heat washing over her, excitement and passion bringing back the wild movements of her body, the incoherent murmurs of joy, the yearning little demands for his possession. It was all gone, her icy wall of fear—love had swept it aside, crushed it, and love took her on flying wings to the midnight sky as Ross claimed her.

'Helen!' His breathing was heavy and uneven as he finally lay against her. 'The way you make me feel is impossible to describe.' He lifted his head to look into eyes that shone with happiness, his hand tracing her face, gently pushing back her damp hair. 'My ice-cold little wife,' he laughed shakily, 'you set me completely on fire.'

Helen cuddled against him, satisfied, content, and across the snowy fields the bells began to ring.

'It's a new year,' she whispered, happy tears flooding her eyes when she thought of what life had been like without him.

He kissed away the tears, knowing perfectly well what they were, as he knew everything about her. 'This is the year when you forget what fear is, forget what unhappiness is. This is the year when Tansy gets a sister.'

'Or a brother,' she whispered, smiling into his eyes, her own eyes wonderfully blue.

'Or a brother,' he agreed tenderly. 'Happy New Year, my darling.

His arms tightened around her, his lips finding her own, and Helen melted against him, two bodies that yearned together, two hearts that beat as one, perfect love and perfect happiness to face a brand-new life.

HARLEQUIN PRESENTS®

A Year Down Under

Beginning in January 1993, some of Harlequin Presents's most exciting authors will join us as we celebrate the land down under by featuring one title per month set in Australia or New Zealand.

Intense, passionate romances, these stories will take you from the heart of the Australian outback to the wilds of New Zealand, from the sprawling cattle and sheep stations to the sophistication of cities like Sydney and Auckland.

Share the adventure—and the romance— of A Year Down Under!

Don't miss our first visit in HEART OF THE OUTBACK by Emma Darcy, Harlequin Presents #1519, available in January wherever Harlequin Books are sold.   YDU-G

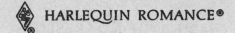

HARLEQUIN®

THE TAGGARTS OF TEXAS!

Harlequin's Ruth Jean Dale brings you
THE TAGGARTS OF TEXAS!

Those Taggart men—strong, sexy and hard to resist...

You've met Jesse James Taggart in FIREWORKS!
Harlequin Romance #3205 (July 1992)

And Trey Smith—he's THE RED-BLOODED YANKEE!
Harlequin Temptation #413 (October 1992)

Now meet Daniel Boone Taggart in SHOWDOWN!
Harlequin Romance #3242 (January 1993)

And finally the Taggarts who started it all—in LEGEND!
Harlequin Historical #168 (April 1993)

Read all the Taggart romances!
Meet all the Taggart men!

Available wherever Harlequin Books are sold.